MUTANT APOCALYPSE

NOW AVAILABLE AND COMING SOON FROM OPEN CASKET PRESS

RATS
HEADSHOTS ONLY
ATOMIC ZOMBIES
ASHES IN HER EYES
ZOMBIE BUFFET
DEAD OFFERINGS
BIGFOOT TALES
HORROR CARNIVAL
CREATURE FEATURE
DEAD CHRISTMAS
DECAY: A ZOMBIE STORY
WOMEN OF THE LIVING DEAD
ZOMBIE BED & BREAKFAST (ZEE BEE & BEE)
HORROR TALES AND TERRIFYING STORIES
2012 ZOMBIE WALL CALENDAR
HOLLOW POINT: A ZOMBIE NOVEL
UNDER A RED SUN: A ZOMBIE NOVEL
WARRIORS OF THE APOCALYPSE: BOOK 1

MUTANT APOCALYPSE

EDITED BY
ANTHONY GIANGREGORIO

Table of Contents

ISLAND GETAWAY

DANIEL LOUBIER

Ten-year-old Sylvia DaSilva lazily pushed a sausage link across her plate with a fork. She looked on with disinterest as her family hungrily ate their breakfast. Her older brother, Bobby, was hunched over his side of the table as he tore into his French toast as if it were the only meal he'd had in five days.

Her father, George, also sat, back rolled forward, eyes-down, repeatedly stabbing at a large stack of pancakes, as if hoping to finish before the Caribbean air had a chance to cool his food. Sylvia's mother, Joanne, however, sat lady-like—straight and proper—just like always. She'd been working on eating a vegetable omelet that looked a bit runnier than it should have, but she didn't seem to be affected by it. Sylvia's meal consisted of scrambled eggs, two sausage links and hash browns.

Everything smelled great when their food had been brought to their table, but Sylvia had lost her appetite as soon as she saw that *thing* with two mouths drool into her orange juice.

"What's the matter, Syl?" George asked through a mouthful of pancakes. "Eat. Your eggs are going to get cold."

Sylvia shrugged her shoulders, apathetic toward anything regarding her meal. It had already been spoiled.

"You better eat it quick," George teased. "Otherwise Bobby's going to take your plate after he's finished with his French toast!"

A chuckle, then a snort came from Bobby.

"Oh, stop, George," Joanne said. "If she's not hungry, she doesn't have to eat." She turned to Sylvia. "Are you not hungry, sweetie?"

Sylvia shook her head.

"Then that's fine. Besides, all our meals are included anyway."

George lowered his head and whispered, "And it ain't like this vacation cost…*an arm and a leg*!" Sylvia rolled her eyes as the three of them coughed, disguising mock laughter.

An arm and a leg. That had been the running joke ever since the use of bio-nuclear weaponry during the 5th World War resulted in unprecedented amounts of mutations, deformations, and abnormalities among humans.

People that had been directly exposed to this kind of warfare had…*changed*. Many people literally lost an arm and/or a leg. Others grew additional appendages, third and fourth eyes, fifteen fingers, multiple penises—those men quickly became popular with the ladies—and so on.

In areas with a high animal population, many people morphed into half-animal/half-human creatures. It wasn't uncommon to see a wild deer, with the head of a man, climbing off the back of a Waste Management truck and emptying the garbage cans in front of your house.

Not surprisingly, most of the world's mutants came from Third World countries. Places like Somalia, Iran, Pakistan and Saudi Arabia had been hit the hardest with bio-nuclear bombs and other weapons of mass destruction. Therefore, those countries accounted for most of the cases of mutation.

The United States also endured its fair share of cases. They hadn't experienced as much as other countries, but that's when the U.S. saw an opportunity. After the FTMPA—Fair Trade of Mutated Persons Act—was established, countries were able to engage in the trade of mutants in exchange for money, goods, and other services. Ever the capitalist nation, the U.S. government, spent millions of dollars to bring in other countries' mutants and put them to work as janitors, garbage men, public restroom attendants, and city bus drivers. Those mutants who weren't too unsightly were able to take on more visible roles, such as waiters in restaurants, sales clerks in department stores, and as receptionists in corporate buildings.

One major change that occurred was that people could no longer have animals as pets. You couldn't even wear a shirt with an animal print, nor have an animal-like doll or object of any kind. This was because the half-human/half-animal mutants retained their natural animal instinct to mate. It wasn't long after the initial mutation 'boom' that people figured this out.

While relaxing in her home, a high-profile business woman wearing a t-shirt that read, **Kruger National Park**, and featuring a picture of a tiger on it, was attacked and molested by her mutant assistant. Another case that made national headlines was of a family that woke up one morning to find their mutant servant sitting on the floor of the kitchen, smoking a cigarette, the family dog lying next to it in a pool of blood after being savagely raped and murdered.

It got so bad that people couldn't even talk about animals. Even the slightest mention of an animal within earshot of a 'humanimal' could trigger a dangerous and potentially deadly situation.

Pictures of animals were prohibited, too. You couldn't so much as put a bumper sticker on a car that read, *I love my Chihuahua*. So a ban was placed on having domesticated animals. That meant no more dogs, cats, no turtles, frogs…not even stuffed, plush animals for the children.

The DaSilva family had only arrived at the island the day before, but already Sylvia was counting the days until they could return to their home in Chicago.

Joanne reached below the table and brought her purse into her lap. She pulled out a handful of brochures and started to poll the family. "Okay, so we can go see some ruins, go hang gliding, ride a mile-long zip line, go snorkeling…what do you guys feel like doing today?"

Bobby smirked. "I think our waiter feels like *doing* our old Golden Retriever," he whispered. He spit out flecks of French toast as he laughed.

"Bobby!" Joanne chided. "I don't want to hear that kind of talk!"

"Sorry."

The two-mouthed individual had brought them their meal, but the mutant that had taken their order was a dog-headed creature that spoke with a Texas accent. Ironically, Sylvia, who'd been brought up in a world where mutants were part of society, and having never met a person from Texas, found his accent to be equally as strange as his man-dog appearance.

"Well, I vote for ruins," Joanne said, and then lowered her voice. "But what I'd *really* like to do is some horseback riding."

"Ha!" Bobby shouted. "Boys don't go hor…" George reached out a hand and cupped Bobby's mouth.

"Robert Anthony DaSilva!" Joanne hissed. "You know you can't talk out loud about…" She looked left and right before whispering, "*Animals!*"

George released his hand from Bobby's mouth. "You apologize to your mother!"

"Sorry, Mom."

Joanne inhaled deeply, smoothed the front of her light yellow Henley t-shirt, and regained her composure. She turned to Sylvia. "What do you want to do, sweetie?"

Sylvia shrugged, her lips curled downward.

"What's wrong, Syl?"

She took a long time before responding. "Nothing."

"Do you want to talk about it?" Joanne asked.

Sylvia shook her head.

"Would you rather write about it?"

Sylvia nodded yes.

"Okay, sweetie, why don't you take out your journal and a pencil and you can write about it. Okay?"

Sylvia nodded again. As she reached beneath her chair for her mini-purse, the waiter returned to the table.

"Hey, y'all! How's everybody doing?" the man-dog creature asked.

"Fine," George said curtly. "We're all fine. Thank you."

"Can I getcha's somethin' else?"

"Nope," George said. "We're all set. Thank you." He spoke fast in an attempt to shoo the mutant away, but it was of no use.

The waiter looked down toward Sylvia. "Aww, shucks, it looks like ya done haven't eaten' a thing? Would you like somethin' else, lil' darlin'?"

Sylvia shook her head silently as she straightened in her chair, and brought a pencil and a notebook onto the table.

"Are you sure? I think we have s…"

Then the world came to a halt. No one spoke. No one moved. They all stared.

At Sylvia, who was oblivious to what she now held in her hand. An eraser in the shape of a poodle attached at the end of her pencil. George swallowed hard, and audibly, as he gazed at the small dog eraser.

"Sylvia? Honey?" he said softly.

Sylvia had already begun to write, but looked up at her father.

"Can you put that away, hon?"

Sylvia looked at the pencil in her hand. At first, she didn't see it. Then her eyes went upward and she found the eraser at the top.

She froze. Her eyes slowly looked up at the waiter. He stared at the eraser. His Siberian husky snout was moist, and he salivated from an open, panting mouth. He licked his jowls twice and his eyes became large.

Suddenly, he stopped panting and a deep, low growl formed in his throat.

"Put your pencil down, Syl," Joanne whispered. "Slowly."

Sylvia carefully lowered the pencil to the table. Tears had formed in her eyes. Two and three at a time, they splashed onto her trembling hand like tiny raindrops.

A man with four arms and fish gills on each side of his neck, presumably the head waiter, walked up next to the man-dog waiter.

"Is everything okay here?"

Man-dog turned quickly and faced Fish-gills. He lowered his shoulders and arched his back, seeming ready to attack his superior.

"Whoa, easy now! Down, boy!" Fish-gills commanded, but Man-dog hunched down even further, as if ready to pounce. "I said, *down!*"

By now, every person at every table in the restaurant had turned their attention toward the disturbance happening at the DaSilva table. Whispers began to reach Sylvia's ears:

"I think the kid has an animal…"

"I think they offended him…"

"Oh my God, is he going to eat the little girl?"

And then it was on.

Man-dog launched off his feet, straight at Fish-gills. They tumbled together onto the floor, and continued to fight as other restaurant guests attempted to get out of the way. With no hesitation, George leaped from his chair. "Come on, let's go!" he called to his family.

George grabbed Bobby's hand, Joanne grabbed Sylvia's, and the four of them ran away from the quarrel on the floor, straight into the panic that had now spread throughout the restaurant.

In a show of posterity, every nearby mutant began attacking the guests, as well as each other. The four of them ran between, and into, other frantic resort patrons. Sylvia looked up. The surreal scene of utter bedlam—mutants fighting with other mutants, people holding on to their loved ones as the freaks of nature tried to take them away, tables and chairs tossed over in frenzied defense—and the sound of pandemonium disappeared into a high-pitched ringing. The noise had risen to such a degree that Sylvia's ears could no longer discern one sound from another. It had all combined into a single steady chime.

Sylvia's father ran ahead, hunched forward, one hand held above his head for protection, and the other held tightly onto Bobby's. Joanne ducked down and stayed close to George, creating a tiny human bubble of protection around Bobby.

Sylvia remained behind. She held on to Joanne's hand and tried to run as fast as her mother, but her feet couldn't keep up.

As confusion continued to ring in her head, Sylvia felt one of her feet become tangled with the other. She lost her grip on Joanne's hand, fell to the floor, and skidded along the tiles on her stomach. When her body came to a stop, she turned over, and saw Man-dog. The mutant was on all-fours, running right at her.

Ten feet away.

She kicked her legs out of instinct. She hit nothing but air, but hoped to catch the mutant where it counted when it finally reached her.

Five feet away.

She kicked even more wildly, as if she were a beast herself, possessed by some strange, animal-like voracity. She imagined she might die by the hands of that monster, but refused to go easily.

Two feet away.

From out of nowhere, her father's body flew over the top of her, colliding with the raging mutant, sending Man-dog off-balance into an overturned table. As if in slow-motion, Joanne's arm came into view above Sylvia. She grabbed at Sylvia's outstretched hands and pulled her up.

Sylvia found her feet quickly and ran behind her mother toward the exit. She looked back quickly and saw George wrestling with Man-dog as she escaped with the rest of her family.

When they reached the door, she looked back one last time. The mutant waiter held her father up off the floor, pinching his arms to his sides. Man-dog's mouth was open, exposing sharp, bloodied teeth. It lunged forward, and just as it was about to close its jaws on George's head, more human-mutant altercations moved into Sylvia's view, blocking her line of sight to her father.

Joanne grabbed Sylvia by both arms and tried to get her attention. Sylvia turned toward her mother and stared at Joanne's mouth as it opened and closed rapidly. The ringing din of anarchy began to subside, intermingling with the renewed sounds of glass breaking, screams, shouts and other large, heavy objects being thrown around.

Eventually, Joanne's voice broke through the cacophony. "Sylvia! We need to go!"

Sylvia looked out along the resort beach. The restaurant was suddenly behind her and she stood outside, on the sand. Her brother was standing in an ocean kayak by the water.

"Bobby and I found boats!" Joanne urged. "Come on! We have to get out of here!"

"What about Daddy?" The innocence with which she posed the question tore at Joanne's heart. Her eyes became bloated with tears that filled quickly, and then emptied over flushed cheeks.

"He's coming, sweetie. Now let's go."

Sylvia felt that Joanne might be lying, but she grabbed her mother's hand and they ran across the beach. Joanne jumped into a kayak and instructed Bobby and Sylvia to ride tandem in another one. Sylvia and her brother climbed into a two-seater. Bobby picked up an oar and began to push the kayak away from the shore while Joanne grabbed another oar, and simultaneously, she and Bobby pushed at the stubborn sand.

"Joanne!"

The three of them looked up. They all recognized the voice and dropped their oars. George had emerged from the restaurant. He slumped over and stumbled onto the sand, then fell to his knees, grabbing at his midsection.

Joanne caught a foot on the side of her kayak and nearly fell into the water as she sprung from the small boat. She raced up the beach and met her husband. He was having trouble breathing.

"Where are you hurt!" she asked.

George groaned as Joanne put her arms around his waist. He continued to clutch at his abdomen, and she immediately saw the blood that thickly coated his hands and lower arms. She pried one of his hands away from his body, ducked under his arm, and carried him toward the water.

"Kids!" she yelled out as she helped George into the kayak. "Your father and I are going to have to share one. He can't row so I'll row for both of us. You two just stay close to me. Okay?"

Bobby and Sylvia nodded.

Sylvia couldn't help but stare at her doubled-over father, as he climbed into the kayak. As hard as he tried to keep all of his blood from spilling out of his body and into the sea, he couldn't stop the flow. Long shoestrings of red weaved through his fingers and into the water as he awkwardly rolled himself into the small water-craft. Joanne held him by the shoulders and made sure he was in completely before getting in the back seat.

"Okay kids, stay close!" Joanne rowed away from shore. Bobby and Sylvia paddled hard to get away from the beach. Bobby, who was older and stronger, sat in the back.

"You row on the left side and I'll row on the right," he told Sylvia.

"Okay."

The four of them stayed close to the shore as they escaped from the resort. Broken waves moved in and lightly tossed the kayaks from side to side. Sylvia stared ahead at her parents' kayak, then farther ahead as the horizon pivoted back and forth at slightly opposite angles.

She took a moment to look back at the resort. By now, the fracas had moved outside. She was too far away and could no longer tell mutant from human. All she saw was a disjointed ballet. A frenzied, choreographed battle of performers, in fits of rage, each of which seeking to overcome the other.

It was beautiful, in a way. And yet, she was relieved to no longer be a part of it.

Ahead of them, Sylvia saw parts of the beach that were much calmer, more peaceful. She didn't see people fighting and tearing each other apart. People played volleyball in the sand and children built sand castles. Farther out on the water, vacationers enjoyed jet skis. She remembered a time, days before they were to leave, when this vacation was supposed to be…a vacation. But now she found herself in a kayak, paddling for her life, along with her brother. She hoped they could stop soon when arms became tired.

"Sylvia, you have to keep rowing!" Bobby yelled from behind when Sylvia rested her oar in her lap.

"Keep up, kids!" Joanne yelled from in front. "We're almost there!"

Almost where? Sylvia thought, as she grabbed the oar and started to paddle again. She looked back one last time. She could no longer see the resort. They had rowed quite a distance already. She wondered if people at another resort might be able to help them. Would there be other, safer mutants? Or would they all attack her and her family the same way the others did.

Joanne rowed her and George's kayak up onto the sand, and Bobby steered his toward the shore. He and Sylvia paddled until the front of the kayak dug into the soft ground. A huge, sweeping hotel stood before them, just beyond the beach. Sylvia estimated at least thirty floors. A giant pool sat between her and the rear of the resort.

Joanne had already gotten herself and George out of the kayak. She swung one of his arms around her and helped him walk.

"Stay with me, kids. We need to get your father some help."

Sylvia and Bobby jumped out of the kayak and stayed close behind. A man, who had likely seen them arrive from the water, ran from the pool area and met them on the sand. He was wearing a white-collared shirt with blue uniform shorts. By all accounts, he looked normal. *Like a human*, Sylvia thought.

The man tossed a brown, circular tray to the ground. "Oh my God, is he okay?"

"No, he's not," Joanne said. "He needs help. Can you get help?"

The man reached an arm under George's shoulder and nodded toward the hotel. "This way, please," he urged. There was no hesitation in his voice, only the sound of genuine concern. Sylvia heard it and felt safe. Secure. She was sure there were mutants working in this resort, too, but it was highly unlikely they were aware of what was happening almost a mile down the beach.

The man, whose nametag read, *Manuel*, helped Joanne carry George up a small stairway, across the pool area, and into the resort.

"What room are you in?" he asked.

"We're not staying here," Joanne panted. "We're down at the Oasis."

Manuel nodded. "I'll have someone call down to the hotel to let them kno…"

Joanne grabbed his arm. "No! You can't!"

Manuel looked back at her in surprise. He studied her briefly. "Okay. That's fine."

Sylvia watched Manuel's face. His eyes darted back and forth, as if confused, trying to put together the mystery around their appearance. Manuel and Joanne carried George across the lightly-colored marble floor of the hotel lobby. George could no longer stand and his feet dragged limply behind. His sandals traced a steady, white stripe through his own blood trail as his life fluid oozed and dripped from his stomach.

Sylvia looked around, nervous about seeing more mutants. To her surprise, there were none. Everyone looked human. Even the people in hotel uniforms looked completely normal. As nervous as she was for her father's safety, she let out a sigh of relief that they were surrounded by only humans.

Manuel yelled something in Spanish across the lobby and three men jumped over a reservation counter. A fourth grabbed a telephone and dialed quickly. When Manuel and Joanne reached the main entrance to the hotel, they laid George on the floor. Manuel ran around the counter and spoke quietly to another hotel employee. Joanne knelt down at George's side and clutched his hand.

"It's okay, baby. You're going to be okay. Help is coming," she whispered.

Sylvia stared at her father's wounds in disbelief. Her parents never let her watch violent movies or TV shows, and she was shocked by how much blood there was. It was like all the blood in her father's body wanted to come out. Having not even considered the worst-case scenario, she wondered how his body would get all that blood back inside it.

Manuel reappeared and squatted next to George, opposite Joanne. "One of my coworkers called the paramedics. They should be here soon." As he said it, a white-and-red van pulled up just outside the front entrance. The word **AMBULANCIA** was written on the side. Two men, wearing white-and-blue shirts with large red crosses on their chests, jumped from the vehicle, removed a stretcher from the back, and hurried into the hotel.

The lead paramedic shouted something in Spanish. Manuel nodded and translated for Joanne. "Okay, ma'am. You will need to move now. Yes?"

Joanne stood and backed away from her husband. The two paramedics, sharing more dialogue in Spanish, placed the stretcher on the ground next to George. They continued to communicate as they quickly assessed his injuries.

"They say it is a lot of blood," Manuel said. "But it looks much worse than it really is."

"Oh, thank God!" Joanne gasped.

Sylvia watched as the paramedics quickly moved George from the floor to the stretcher, then carried him out to the ambulance. Joanne began to follow, but Manuel placed a hand on her arm.

"You cannot ride in ambulance with him, but I know which hospital he will be going to. I will have a taxi take you there immediately."

Joanne nodded. She squatted down and hugged Bobby and Sylvia, held them both close.

"Your father's going to be okay," she said, wiping at her eyes. "He's going to be fine."

Despite Joanne's words, Sylvia remained unsure. She stared back at Joanne, stoic, and tried to read something in her mother's face, something Joanne wasn't telling Sylvia and her brother. But there was nothing there. Joanne believed George was going to be okay.

"Ma'am?" Manuel said.

"We're leaving?" Joanne asked expectantly.

"Yes, in one minute, ma'am. But first, there is something I need to tell you."

"Oh no!" Joanne cried. "Is it George? Did the paramedics say something else? Is he going to be okay?"

"Yes, ma'am, your husband will be fine. But, one of my co-workers, he call down to your hotel…"

Manuel paused for a moment. His eyes appeared slightly less compassionate than before. His eyebrows straightened, as if he was glaring. "We understand there was an…*incident* at your hotel." When he said the word, his lips peeled back briefly to reveal razor-sharp teeth.

Then Manuel's body began to contort. His arms and legs shifted position, his waist expanded, and his legs spread out on either side.

His arms lowered toward his midsection and four more legs grew out. Sylvia heard cracking and snapping like twigs and branches, as the new appendages extended from his body, leaving his upper torso suspended like a spider.

Sylvia looked around to see that all of the hotel employees were transforming now. Some morphed into half-human/half-insect creatures.

Others removed their clothes, revealing hidden limbs, claws, wings and other deformities. Sylvia grabbed onto her mother's waist as the mutants closed in on her, Joanne and Bobby.

When Sylvia turned to face Manuel again, she saw that each of his legs was covered with short, spindly black hair.

He crawled closer to Joanne and Bobby, then lifted one of his spider legs and placed it on Joanne's shoulder.

"It seems *someone* doesn't know how to follow the rules." He shot a quick glance at Sylvia.

"She didn't know," Joanne begged. "I promise! She didn't do it on purpose!"

Sylvia looked around again. She and her family were surrounded now.

She couldn't see past the circle of hotel employees, and was unable to catch sight of any humans around to help her or her family.

It wouldn't matter anyway.

"It's too late for breakfast," Manuel began. "And too early for lunch." His eyes widened and his lips curled up into a psychotic grin. "But I think there's room for a light snack."

STANDOFF AT POOCHY'S

DAVID BERNSTEIN

Scott awoke to blood-curdling screams. There was no need to think. He grabbed his sidearm, a Colt .45 model M1911, and ran out of the tent. Camp had been made along the edge of the mountain where the trees were scarce and huge rock slabs took up most of the ground. The moon was full, illuminating the area well. Scott and the others had learned to hate when the moon was full, the far away sphere seeming to cause the mutants to act crazier than they normally did.

"Cathy and Joan's tent," Rob said, pointing in their direction. He had his SKS rifle in hand.

Two large, pale feet, with talons for toes, were protruding from the women's tent.

Rob raised his rifle, then stopped. He might wind up hitting one of the girls. And if there were any more mutants in the area, they'd come running. Dropping the rifle, he bent down and grabbed the mutant's ankles, pulling the creature out.

"Cathy!" he yelled, but received no reply.

"We'll get to her," Scott said, squatting next to his buddy, taking up an ankle. Together they yanked the disfigured man from the tent. The thing was naked and grunting like a wild animal. It clawed at the ground, wanting more of what it had already tasted—its blood-covered hands and mouth a dead giveaway that one or both women were injured. Or worse, dead.

Rob struggled to hold the mutant down, sitting on its legs, while Scott climbed onto its back. Pulling his machete from its sheath, he raised it up, point down, and sank the blade into the back of the monster's neck, just below the skull. Most mutants were strong and built like mini tanks, the bones calcifying and making it hard to kill them unless struck in a tender area like the neck, groin, or abdomen. The head and upper chest were like steel and were almost impenetrable regions.

The creature fell still almost immediately, with only its limbs twitching, as if it had touched an exposed electrical outlet. Scott wondered how the hell it had gotten so close without anyone hearing it. Mutants were noisy, always grunting and screaming like wild boars.

Rob jumped up, wanting to rush inside and see if his love was still alive. "Cathy!" he shouted.

Scott held him back.

Rob's teeth were clenched, his eyes full of rage and fear. "Let me go, Scott!"

"I know," Scott said, "but let me go first. You don't need to see if…"

"Don't say it," Rob said, cutting him off. "Don't you dare. She's alive."

"Okay," Scott said. "But neither one's answering. Wait here and keep an eye out for any other uglies."

Scott turned toward the tent and swallowed, but the lump in his throat refused to go down. There was so much blood pooling around the tent. At least one of the women was dead. He was sure of it.

"Do you hear anything?" Rob asked, angrily. "Any charging or howling *mutees*?"

"No."

"That's because there are no others."

"Well, this one managed to get inside a tent with no one the wiser, so keep an ear out while I do this."

They were lucky that it was just the one mutant. If there'd been a pack of the ugly things, they most likely would've all been slaughtered. Ripped apart and eaten.

The group had become lax during their time in the walled-in village, and when they headed for the mountains. Brooklyn—Scott, Rob, and Cathy's original place of living—had been hell, having to hide and keep quiet in an apartment building for months. Finally, after the mutants breached their home, the group had no choice but to hightail it out of there. They found a car and took a chance.

They made it out of the city unscathed and drove north after seeing a sign with the words, **A New Beginning: Head To Crown Point N.Y.** They'd found a map in an abandoned gas station and worked their way to the small farming town where a walled-in village awaited.

A year after having been there, living a relatively fine life, a heavily-armed gang of thirty humans came through and destroyed the place. Many were killed or taken. Scott, Rob, Cathy and another woman, Joan, were out hunting at the time of the onslaught, and it was just simple luck that had most likely kept them alive.

During the time in the village, the group had learned basic, and some advanced, survival skills—learning to live off the land, and what nature provided. Gathering, fishing, and hunting became a staple in their daily lives.

Using the machete, Scott pulled back a large portion of the slashed fabric and poked his head into the tent. The inside of the tent walls were painted a glistening red. Body parts lay scattered in a sea of blood. Scott closed his eyes, needing a moment, then resumed his search and began moving the flashlight's beam around. A leg moved and he jumped. He hadn't expected anyone to be alive.

"Talk to me, Scott," Rob said, his voice sounding ready to crack.

"Give me a sec," he said to Rob, then looked back inside.

"Cathy, babe? You okay?" Rob called over Scott's shoulder.

"Keep quiet," Scott whispered. "There might be more mutees out there." He stepped inside the tent and felt his gorge rise, then pinched his nose to avoid the heavy, metallic odor. "Cathy?" he called out. No reply. Hunched over, he stepped forward toward the leg he saw move ever so slightly and almost lost his balance when he stepped on a severed hand. The leg belonged to Cathy.

She was lying at the back of the eight foot tall, ten foot wide tent, her body pressed up against the fabric, her eyes wide open in shock and fear, her chest rising and falling quickly. She was caked in blood and pieces of flesh, as if a blender had been put on puree with the top off and then she had been doused with the remaining contents. Scott couldn't tell if she was wounded, or if it was pieces of Joan, but she was alive—her expanding and contracting chest an indication.

"Rob," he called.

"Yeah."

"Cathy's alive, but I can't tell if she's hurt. Go around back. I'm going to slice a hole for us to push her through. I don't want to drag her through…all of this."

"Okay," Rob said, already moving to the back of the tent.

Scott poked the machete into the fabric and began cutting, making the slit the length of Cathy's body. Once the material fell outward, he could push, and Rob could pull.

Scott tossed the machete through the slit and placed his hands on Cathy's body, while Rob grabbed her from behind. Cathy screamed and began swatting at both men, having gone from a catatonic state to a spastic one.

"She's in shock," Scott said. "Pull her out."

Rob pulled her out of the tent and held her tight against his body so that she couldn't flail around. Her mouth, however, was free to be used. She screamed for a few moments before quieting down and sobbing.

Scott hoped she'd be okay. Cathy was a strong woman, and had seen and been through a lot. But watching a friend get shredded and fed upon before her eyes, while fearing for her own life, had to do something to the psyche.

Scott ran to the nearby stream, filled a pot with water, and carried it back to camp. Rob had started a fire and the water was soon boiling. Cathy's wound looked bad. There were three claw marks, each deep and ragged, as if the skin had been pulled apart instead of sliced, running down her left side just under the arm.

She was in and out of consciousness, but when the boiling water was poured over the wounds, she screamed loud enough to wake the dead. After the water came the rubbing alcohol, which made Cathy scream even louder than the boiling water did. Eventually, she passed out from the pain as the two men finished bandaging her wounds using duct tape and a shredded shirt. She lost some blood and the wound looked like it would need stitches, but for now the tape and material would have to do. The two men carried her back to their tent and placed her in a sleeping bag.

Sitting outside the tent, Rob asked Scott if he thought she'd be all right.

"No idea," Scott said. "I'm far from a doctor and that wound looked bad. But she's strong. We'll have to go into a nearby town and get a needle and thread. That tape won't hold for long."

"We're almost out of tape, too."

"Well, she's patched up for now. As soon as she's able, we'll head out. A day or two. And if not, then one of us will have to go alone. I guess it'll be me. You'll need to stay with her. Going into a town is a good idea anyway. Hopefully we'll find some medical supplies. We have to get her sewn up."

"We need to start collecting bottles and cans again," Rob said. "For the trip wires." He picked up a small stone and tossed it away angrily. "I can't believe we didn't set up some kind of perimeter."

"Yeah—we really got lazy living in that village. Those people were too content, thinking they could just start over and all would be well. They forgot that even in these times people are still fucked up."

"That gang was well-armed and malicious. They would've slaughtered them, us, whether the villagers were prepared or not."

"Maybe, but at least it would've been a fight and not a slaughter."

"Damn it, we had it good there for a while."

Scott didn't like dwelling on the past. Yes, it had been good, but they'd had it even better before the damn plague, too. No use in fretting about it. Move on. Survive. Live.

"Let's go take down that tent and make a grave for Joan."

Scott and Rob rose early the next day, getting only about four hours of sleep. They needed to pack up just in case Cathy would be okay to leave. The next town could be close, or far. With no map of the area, and the nearer towns having been cleaned out by the villagers, they would be traveling blind.

Leaving the mountain area wasn't something Scott wanted to do. He and the others had enjoyed the quiet, and had learned to live off the land, and had done so nicely. But with winter approaching in a few months, they needed to find shelter and supplies, and finding goods was a crap shoot. About one percent of the human population was unaffected by the plague, leaving numerous towns filled with supplies for the taking. Yes, many places, especially the big cities, were raided or packed with mutees, but a lot of smaller towns and hamlets had store shelves that lay untouched.

Rob wanted to wake Cathy but Scott figured it best to let her wake on her own. If by nightfall she was still sleeping, then he would get her up. Her wound needed to be kept clean and fresh tape and cloth would need to be applied. As it was, the tape was holding but the wounds were still bleeding through, causing the tape to come loose. Being out on the road, and making runs into unknown areas, could prove dangerous. Cathy would need to be okay before doing so or she had to stay behind.

Scott and Rob sat by the campfire, cooking up slices of deer meat, having smoked a large amount to take with them on the road. It was late afternoon, about four hours before sunset. Hopefully, they'd all be able to leave the next day, or Scott would have to set out on his own—at least until he found a needle and thread. He didn't want to think about the wound getting infected. If that happened, they'd have to find a town with a drugstore that hadn't been raided. Good luck with that.

"Hey," Cathy said, walking over from the tent.

"You're up," Rob responded enthusiastically. He looked at Scott. "Good sign," he said, then stood up to meet his girlfriend. He stopped short of embracing her. "You're really bloody. She's really bleeding, Scott."

Scott saw the blood, but it wasn't as bad as he thought it could have been. The duct tape was doing a pretty good job.

"It's to be expected," he said. "Stop freaking the girl out."

"What happened?" Cathy said.

"You don't remember?" Rob asked.

"Of course I remember, but why am I bleeding so much and why doesn't it seem to bother Scott?"

Rob led Cathy to a spot by the fire and sat next to her. "You have a few large gashes down your side. That mutee clawed you good. You're going to need stitches."

"And possibly antibiotics," Scott added. "But the tape and wads of shirt are okay for now it seems. Just don't do a lot of anything."

"It hurts like a bitch," she complained.

"A combination of pain from the wound and pain from cleaning it I suppose," Scott said. "Hopefully it'll feel a little better tomorrow."

"How are you feeling otherwise, babe?" Rob asked. "Head woozy? Any nausea?"

"My head's clear, and the pain is keeping me focused I think. I'm not nauseous or anything—just a little weak. It's the pain that's the worst, but I'll manage." She paused a moment, then looked at Scott. "You're worried about infection setting in, aren't you."

Scott flipped the pieces of deer meat over with a pair of tongs. "It's possible that the wound is infected, but we did do a thorough job of cleaning it."

"We burned the shit out of it," Rob said. "Boiling water and rubbing alcohol."

"Burn it again, but use something metal. Singe the flesh together. Infection nowadays is a death sentence," she said, clearly unnerved.

"We already cleaned it as best we could. The skin won't melt together. We need to find a needle and thread."

"Screw the stitches. I don't want to wait. Just cauterize the damn thing."

"Babe," Rob began. "No way. It would kill you."

"No faster than an infection without antibiotics would."

"The wounds are too deep and too long. Rob's right; the pain alone would probably kill you. Let's not worry about that. If we need to get to a pharmacy, we'll find one," Scott said.

"Come on," Cathy said. "They've all been raided by now."

"Not true," Rob added. "We found one in Brooklyn of all places. Remember?"

"True, but it's a year later," she said.

"We're in the countryside. I'm sure there are plenty of towns that haven't been cleaned out yet, along with some homes. We'll find drugs if we need to. It's the needle and thread that's most important now. You're not losing a lot of blood yet, but over time the amount you lose will add up; and if the tape becomes useless and the wounds don't heal…"

"Okay," Cathy said. "I get it."

It was quiet for a moment, only the crackle of the fire heard. Finally, Cathy said,

"Joan…where is she?"

Scott and Rob looked at each other.

"I mean…what did you do with her…her body?"

"We buried her," Scott said. "A ways out from here."

"Take me there. I need to say goodbye."

"Okay, sure. First thing tomorrow," Rob said. "Tonight you need to rest up."

"We all do," Scott echoed. "We've got a long journey ahead of us." He wasn't sure how well Cathy was going to be able to travel, but it looked like it was going to be a see-as-they-go venture.

That evening, Scott and Rob swapped guard duty, letting Cathy sleep through the night. She woke a couple of times in pain, the wound making it hard to sleep.

Just after sunrise the next morning, Rob took Cathy to Joan's grave. The grave had been dug using the one camping shovel the group had. It was hard going, but Scott and Rob wanted the woman to have a proper place of burial. The world might not care about its living, but it still had people in that did, and part of being human was honoring the dead.

The grave wasn't too deep. A collection of stones had been found and placed atop the packed dirt to keep the wildlife away.

Cathy knelt by Joan's eternal resting place, said a few words, then rose to her feet. "I didn't know her that well, but she was a strong person. It could've been her or me in that tent. Her or me."

Rob was glad it was Joan and not Cathy. It was a cold, harsh thought, but one he knew was the truth. "Luck of the draw," was all he said.

When they returned to camp, Scott had already packed up everything. They put on their backpacks, including Cathy with some assistance, grabbed their mountain bikes, and rode down the mountain.

Traveling in an automobile was good when a person knew where he was going, but when the destination was unknown, non-motorized modes of transport were the best idea. Noise was the number one way to attract mutants, as well as other humans. The group didn't want to run into either—not after witnessing how horrendous humans could be.

They didn't know how far they would have to travel. If they knew where they were going, they could grab a vehicle—as cars were in abundance, the vehicles having been abandoned everywhere—and just park a ways away from their destination. Driving into a town filled with mutants was pointless. The streets would fill, making the town anything but habitable. So bicycles it was.

The road they traveled was a one lane, back country affair with little in the way of steep hills. The nearest town was Portsmouth, but it was virtually void of any supplies—the walled-in villagers having raided the place some time ago. But there were numerous small towns dotting the landscape and the group was sure they'd find one untouched by raiders. Mutants would be another story, but they'd deal with that when they had to.

Two hours into the journey, with Cathy holding up well, Scott stopped pedaling and came to a halt. He stood up with the bike between his legs, looking down the road.

"What's up?" Rob asked, but then he saw it.

Cathy too.

Something was in the middle of the road about fifty feet ahead of them, a lump of some kind.

"Damn, I wish we had binoculars," Rob said.

"Yeah," Scott agreed. "Remember that when we hit the next town."

"I'll put it on the shopping list."

The group had their guns at the ready as well as other, quieter weapons. Scott had his machete, Rob his metal-studded baseball bat, and Cathy her Samurai sword, although she didn't think she could do much swinging in her condition. The pain she thought she could withstand. It was the pealing-off of the duct tape that she couldn't risk. The wound, since last night, had almost stopped bleeding, with a minute amount of seepage.

Walking the bikes up the road, the group approached the lump.

"Help me, please," the lump said.

"Holy shit," Rob gasped.

"Help me," the thing said.

It was a half mutant, half man; a Siamese twin, connected at the waist. The thing wore dirty, ragged jeans and a dingy jacket. The half man part looked like he hadn't washed in years, his hair falling out along with his teeth, of which he had only a few re-maining. The mutant half looked to be dead or sleeping. It was grotesque like most mutants, with huge knobs of toughened flesh on its bald head and face, like giant unpoppable zits. The nose was split and one eye was two inches lower than the other.

"Kill me. Please, kill me. I'm so tired." The man was reaching out with his human arm, the fingernails long, yellowed and caked with dirt.

No one from the group moved.

"You're human…" Scott said, confused.

"I was," the man whispered.

"What can we do?" Scott asked.

"Kill me before *it* wakes up."

Everyone jumped back.

"What do you mean, 'wakes up'?" Rob asked. "That thing's alive?"

The man continued to sob, like he was trying to do so as quietly as possible.

"His name is Hank and he was my brother—before the plague. He turned. I didn't. We've been together like this since it all started. He doesn't hurt me 'cause I'm part of him. I think he knows that killing me will kill him, too. But I can't stand it any more."

"Mister," Scott said. "I don't know what…"

"There's nothing to do. I'm tired of living like this. I loved my brother and every time I've attempted to end our lives he's known about it, and stops me before I can do it. I think he can read my mind. He's not like the other mutants I've come across. He understands things, but it's his rage, like the other mutants, that causes him to act like them. When we're alone, he's tolerable." The man closed his eyes.

Scott didn't know what to do. The man was asking for a mercy killing, having lived his whole life attached to another person—who was now a mutant. He couldn't imagine what it must be like.

The man looked terrible. If it were him he'd want the same he supposed.

"We can't stay out in the open like this," Cathy said quickly.

The man opened his eyes. "Keep your voice down. You'll wake him, and trust me you don't want him joining the conversation."

"Keep an eye out on our surroundings," Scott told her. "Maybe we can use this to our advantage."

"How's that?" Rob asked.

"Mister," Scott said.

The man opened his eyes, and Scott looked into them for the first time. They were haunted, vacant of sanity. Scott felt an unease creep over him, but he held still. This man-mutant might have answers that the group, specifically Cathy, needed.

"How about a trade?" Scott asked.

"Trade? I have nothing as you can see," the man said.

"Are you from these parts? Do you know the area well?"

"I've lived here all my life."

"Give us information and we'll see to your wishes."

"Anything."

"Are there any towns within a day's bike ride from here that haven't been raided?"

The man's eyes lit up. "Yes. Yes. Of course. Many untouched towns. Free for the picking."

"Any of them have a pharmacy?"

"Yes, of course. Almost all towns do, don't they? I'll tell you the way. But please, kill me right after because my brother will wake soon. I think he's hungry."

"Spit it out then," Cathy said in a hushed voice.

"You just keep going down this road. You'll come to Headenville. Don't stop there, it's a mutee town, and was stripped clean—down to the bones—if you know what I mean. After you make it through town, keep on until the first left. You'll see a sign for

Waterhole. That's a really small town, so the mutant population should be easy to deal with, and they have a pharmacy for sure. It's where me and my brother used to go years ago."

"And that's it?" Scott asked.

"Yes. Now, we had a deal."

"Any mutees nearby that you know of?"

"No. Your gunshot won't be heard. We're in the middle of nowhere. I'm only here because I'm a loner." The man chuckled, then motioned to his grotesque other half. "Well, you know what I mean."

"You guys probably don't want to see this," Scott told the others.

"Just do it. We need to get moving," Rob said. "Cathy's not looking so good."

"I'm fine," she said. "Just tired."

Scott held the Beretta out, pointing it at the man. "Ready?"

"Wait," the man said, holding up his arms. "You have to put the gun to my brother's head—shoot him first. He's the one with the grizzly bear-like skull. If I was you, I'd put it right up to his eye. Make sure you scramble his brains like an egg." The man chuckled. "Then do me quick after. I don't want to suffer, to feel his pain, to feel his body take mine with it."

The man was right, Scott knew. The .30-06 or SKS would do the job, but that was overkill on a sitting, unmoving target. He just wanted this over quickly. He'd never killed anyone without good reason—except in self defense. But along with this new, cruel world came new, harsh rules, and when a truly suffering soul, like the man in front of him, asked to be put out of his misery, then he must oblige.

"Hold still," Scott said. "I'll make it swift. I promise."

The man nodded, then looked away as Scott approached and placed the barrel of the gun against the mutee's eyelid. Just as he was about to pull the trigger, the eye opened. At the same time the human side of the mutee grabbed the gun, while the mutee side punched Scott in the gut. In the blink of an eye, the Siamese twins were up, pointing the gun at Scott's head.

"What the fuck?" Rob asked, turning his gun on the mutee.

"I knew it," Cathy said angrily.

"Hehehehehehe," the human side of the mutee proclaimed, keeping the weapon on Scott. He was grinning as if he'd just heard the best news in the world while the mutant part growled, "My brother's hungry." It's voice was a garbled cry.

"Fuck you," Cathy said. "We tried to help you."

"Hehehehe. And so you shall. Come my brothers and sisters," the man called out. "Come forth and join your kings."

"Kings?" Rob said. "What the fuck—is this nutjob crazy or what?"

"I don't think he's crazy," Scott said. "I think he's smart. Very smart indeed."

"Smart I am. Smart I am. A little crazy, sure. Who wouldn't be, but I'm a king. My brother, too. Kings of all the mutants!"

"Bullshit," Rob said.

From the nearby field covered in tall grass that swayed in the breeze, thirty or so mutees jumped up, hollering, and came running toward the group.

"Holy shit!" Rob yelled.

"I'm going to kill this piece of shit," Cathy said, aiming her gun at the twins. "If we're gonna die, then I'll take their kings with us."

"No, no, no. The king wants to stay, and stay he will. Right, brother?" The mutee brother roared and swiped at Scott, who managed to jump out of the way. "Relax, brother, we have to share with the others."

The twin shook his head violently.

"I know you're hungry, but I'm in charge. The first king. You're the second."

The thing shook its head again.

"Okay. We're the kings equally, but I make the rules. I've got the brains."

The mutee seemed to like that. He nodded his head and rubbed his hand against his leg excitedly.

"You sneaky bastard," Scott said. "Playing the victim. But how is it possible you can communicate with those things?"

"Things?" The man asked angrily. "You're the *things*. We're the new race of planet Earth. We've evolved. Your kind is weak and easily killed. Infection, disease—a little blade can easily end your life."

The horde of mutants was fast approaching like a pack of stampeding bulls. If Scott didn't do something soon, they'd all be dead, a meal for the mutants.

"Cathy, Rob," he said. "On three. Silent count."

"What? What are you saying? Be quiet," the human king of mutants said.

Scott counted to three in his head, then ducked really low to the left. It was a routine the group had worked on at the village; a timing strategy when covertness was needed. He heard a shot from his left, Rob's or Cathy's, he wasn't sure. But the bullet hit its intended target. The man-king's head flew back. His arm went limp and the gun dropped to the road.

The mutant twin roared, spittle flying from its mouth as if it had rabies. Scott had the machete out. He was crouched next to the dead twin, the lifeless body acting like a shield. Raising his arm up, he swung at the mutee's neck. He could have jumped away and let Rob and Cathy nail it with bullets, but a chop to the neck, taking the head off, was the best option. The blade only sunk in halfway, coming to a stop when it hit the calcified spinal column.

Knowing the creature was far from dead—at least for now, given time the wound might kill it—Scott hit the ground and yelled for the others to shoot. Gunfire erupted. Bullets hit the mutee, taking off its skull in bits and pieces. Scott scurried away in a crabwalk. Bullets continued to fly, tearing up the creature's neck and abdomen. It came forward, working its way against the onslaught, a trout swimming up-stream.

The thirty mutees were almost to the road. The three humans were as good as dead. Scott didn't want to go out this way—not any way—but ambushed? He and the others had been careless again.

Finally, the Siamese mutee fell to the road, its stomach and neck a pulp of tissue, blood and muscle. Scott jumped up. He wouldn't go out without a fight. He slipped off his pack to grab his .30-06 when Rob and Cathy gasped.

The charging mutants had stopped. The malformed things were on their knees, bowing in the group's direction. No one moved.

"Hey, what's going on?" Rob asked.

"I have no idea."

"I think they think we're the kings now," Cathy said, still pointing her weapon at the bowing mutees. "The old pack mentality. Whoever takes out the current leader is the new boss. The new king."

"And now they've got a queen," Rob said.

"I think you're right, Cathy," Scott agreed.

The mutants rose together almost as one.

"Go," Scott said, authoritatively to the mutee crowd. "Your old kings are dead. We are your new kings. Go back to the forest and wait. We shall bring food soon."

"You've got to be kidding me," Rob whispered.

"Quiet," Cathy hissed.

They watched as the mutants strode back into the field and the forest beyond.

"I can't believe that worked," Rob said, shaking his head. "They understood you."

"These mutees are different," Scott mused. "More evolved than the others we've seen."

"Damn, that's all we need. Smarter mutants."

"This changes things," Scott added.

"Damn straight it does. Now we have to be extra cautious. It explains how that one got in our tent. It must've snuck up, avoided stepping on anything that would make noise, only once it attacked it lost control," Rob said.

"We better get going," Scott said. "There's no telling when those things will come back, or how long they'll treat us as their new kings and queen."

The group hopped on their bikes and rode down the road.

Forty-five minutes later they came upon a large sign with the words, **Welcome to Gamorville** on it. Buildings could be seen about a quarter mile ahead. The bikes were ditched in the woods, along with backpacks. Only weapons would be carried.

The group walked the road into town. A church stood on the immediate left and next to it was the town library. Farther down was a gas station, a McDonald's, and an assortment of other stores no one could make out.

The place seemed deserted but that didn't mean a thing. The mutants could be gathered nearby, or in the buildings. A few windows were broken here and there but from the looks of it, the town was in good condition.

"Let's find the pharmacy and get the hell out of here," Rob said.

One side of Cathy's shirt, where she'd been gouged, was completely saturated in red. The wound had begun bleeding more since the incident with the twins.

Scott saw her noticing it and said, "We'll get you fixed up real soon."

"I see it." Rob was pointing ahead to where a pharmacy stood untouched, the glass windows unbroken.

They continued to move toward the drugstore until a mutant—rather small, but no child—came around the corner of the pharmacy building. It spotted them immediately and began running, arms out and over-sized mouth gaping open—though it only had a few rotting teeth.

"Don't shoot," Scott said, withdrawing the machete from its sheath. But then another mutant came around the corner. This one was huge, easily six feet five inches, wearing only overalls, and built like a tank. Two more mutants appeared seconds later.

"Shit!" Cathy said.

"See if that bar's open and head inside," Scott said, pointing and running in the direction of Poochy's Bar.

Rob got there first. "The door's unlocked." He went in, holding the door for the others.

Once inside, Scott slammed and locked the door. The mutants pounded on it, the wood rattling violently, but holding. If too many more fists began banging, it might not hold for long, given the strength of some of the mutants. Rob and Scott began stacking tables and chairs against the door. Cathy went over to a window and pulled the curtain. There was no way to block the windows but they were high enough off the ground that with luck, the slow-witted mutants wouldn't realize they could simply come in through a window.

"There's two more uglies coming to join the others," she said as she slid the curtain closed.

"Shit," Scott breathed. "Rob, see if there's a way out back. I'll check behind the bar for something we can use."

Rob returned less than thirty seconds later. "The back entrance leads into an alley. Looks clear."

"There's no liquor behind the bar," Scott said, standing by a door leading to the basement. "Follow me."

"What? Why?" Rob asked.

"He's looking for alcohol," Cathy explained, her complexion ghostlike. She felt cold, but wouldn't tell the others. They had enough to worry about.

"To clean her wound with?" Rob asked.

"Just get over here," Scott insisted, and plodded down the stairs.

Looking around the basement, Scott grinned. The shelves were full of liquor: bottles of vodka, gin, rum, bourbon, cases and kegs of beer. If things were only different, he thought, he could throw a party. It might be worth it to stick around and wipe the town clean of mutees just to have the stash before him.

"Holy shit!" Rob gasped as he came down the stairs and saw the liquor.

"Tell me about it."

"Damn, I wish we had a van or a truck and a clear way out of this place."

"Look for anything that'll burn."

The two began grabbing bottles of Bacardi 151, Wild Turkey 101, and Smirnoff Blue Label, along with some 80 proof liquors. All of it would burn, but the 100 proof-and-up alcohol would be the igniter. Each man traveled up and down the stairs to the first floor with bottles in their arms, careful not to drop any.

Finished with the basement, and a nice collection of alcohol before them, Scott said, "Start breaking bottles; we need to douse this place." He pulled off the cap and took a swig, relishing the warmth as it slid down his throat and hit his stomach, then threw a bottle of Bacardi 151 against the entrance door, shattering it. The liquor splashed all over the pile of tables and chairs, which were being jolted from the mutants pounding on the door. "Work your way towards the rear exit."

When all but one bottle—Bacardi 151—remained, the group gathered just outside the rear door in the alley. "Okay, I'll be right back," Scott said, and ran back into the main room of the bar.

He went to one of the front windows, smashed it out with the butt of his rifle, and began screaming. He fired a couple of shots, not at any mutees in particular, just wanting any of the ugly bastards in the area to come running. His plan worked. More and more mutants arrived, from buildings, the woods, and from down the street.

"Almost ready!" he yelled. "Come on, you ugly fucks! I'm right here!"

Disfigured arms, lined with puss-leaking sores, reached through the window. The mutants didn't care as the broken glass gouged their arms. The front door was giving way; the tables and chairs would soon no longer hold. Scott ran to the back, his objective accomplished, and met up with the others.

Rob handed the Molotov cocktail he'd made earlier to Scott.

"Now we wait," he said. "How you doing, Cathy?"

"Hanging in there," she smiled slightly.

"Good. Hand me the lighter."

"She's losing a lot of blood, man," Rob said. "We've got to get her stitched up."

Scott took the lighter and was about to speak when he heard an explosion from inside the bar. The mutees had broken through the door.

"They're inside," he told the others, who had both clearly heard the crash. Rob and Cathy, as planned, began working their way down the alley, leaving Scott to finish the job.

The first mutant charged into the back room, quickly followed by another and another, and like grains of sand, they continued to pour in. Using the lighter, Scott lit the rag jutting from the neck of the bottle, and with a pang of guilt for ruining such a valued bottle of liquor, he tossed it inside. The mutants were onto his presence in a second, and began running his way. He slammed the door closed, and heard the whoosh of the flames erupt as the home-made bomb went off. He ran down the alley, joining Rob and Cathy, who were waiting impatiently.

Together, they made their way to the woods outside of town, watching as the bar went up in flames, black smoke filling the air. A few mutants escaped the fire and were seen running away, walking balls of flame that eventually slowed and collapsed in the street.

After waiting over an hour, only ten more mutants had shown up. It appeared the town was virtually wiped clean of the infected creatures. With their guns blazing like cowboys from the Old West, the trio mowed down the remaining mutants with ease, and quickly made their way to the pharmacy.

The inside of the drugstore wasn't untouched by looters, but the people who had been inside must have been in and out quickly, because most items were still on the shelves. The security gate for the pharmacy section was down and locked, but with a few gunshots to the lock, the gate was able to be opened.

Scott, Rob and Cathy grabbed as many drugs as they could carry, using shopping bags from behind the counter. A first aid kit was found in aisle 4 with a needle and thread, amongst other items they could use. They loaded up on anything that seemed worthy of carrying and then left, closing the door behind them for the next needy travelers.

Even though the town was most likely safe, it wasn't a smart idea to remain in it—for now.

They made their way back to where they'd left the bicycles.

The three survivors made camp a ways into the woods, far enough from the road so that a fire could be had that evening without fear of being seen. Cathy's wounds were cleaned again. The deep scratches didn't appear to be infected—no pus or black veins—but she was given dose of antibiotics just in case. After patching her up, Scott and Rob rode the bikes back into town, leaving Cathy at the camp to rest.

An hour later, they returned with bags full of canned goods, such as baked beans, vegetables, and soda, along with a bunch of preserved cupcake-like snacks.

"Dates aren't good," Scott told Cathy, "but I'm not complaining."

That night the group ate well. They remained in the camp, with daily trips to the town, obtaining more food and supplies. They found books, magazines, and board games, that latter keeping them occupied for the week they stayed at the camp.

On the eighth day, they packed up and moved out. With no destination planned and not knowing how far they would travel, they commandeered a van, hoping to find a place they could one day call home.

BLOB TAG

R P STEEVES

"You're it!" Mildred cried, lunging toward her classmate, missing completely, and tumbling down the rocky slope.

"Missed me!" the other girl yelled, a shrill cry piercing Millie's ears as she scrambled to her feet, the tiniest trickle of blood seeping from a gash in her knee. "Besides," the other girl, Barb was her name, or at least that's what Millie believed, anyway, as the other girl had never bothered to introduce herself, "you're supposed to be frozen, aren't you?"

Millie frowned. She didn't know the girl well enough to tell if she was kidding, and much to her chagrin, their louder than normal discussion was starting to draw a crowd; a swarm of similar-looking girls dressed in similar-looking jumpers all with similar-looking sneers on their faces.

"Wha…but I…uh, my father, he…" Millie stopped to compose herself as her jitters elicited whispered comments from the crowd. "I didn't realize we were playing that version of tag. I don't really like it. My father was frozen alive to keep from being eaten by Joyners, you know."

That evoked full-fledged laughter from many of the girls. "Yeah," snorted Barb, clearly their leader. "We know. Everyone in the compound knows your father smooshed a Joyner." The laughter grew, and Millie could feel her face flush red. Barb walked slowly down the rocky hill so she could stand in front of Millie, a good foot taller than the new girl, even without the benefit of the incline.

"He did not smoosh a Joyner," Millie whispered, her face burning hot now, her eyes tearing up.

"That's not what I heard, Joyner-spawn." Simultaneous with the insult, Barb shot her hand out, shoving Millie harshly on the shoulder. "Your mother was a Joyner-lover. That's why she went crazy." Another shove and Millie's bare feet skidded down the hill, the rocks tearing at her flesh. "I would have, too, if I'd been stuck taking care of you."

Another shove. This time, Millie shoved back.

This was a response that Barb hadn't anticipated. As Millie pushed, Barb's feet dropped out from under her and she stumbled, drawing a gasp from the assembled mob. The girl toppled right onto Millie, which was fine with her. She and her mother had developed some pretty strong survival skills in the Greyness, and those instincts kicked into gear at the moment of contact.

Millie wrestled Barb to the ground, a guttural cry emanating from deep within, her arms and fists flailing against the flanks of her former tormentor. After a moment, Millie felt a mass of hands grab her hair and the back of her jumper, desperately trying to pull her off Barb. As the hands tugged at her, she reached out, grasping onto whatever she could to keep herself from being yanked away. In this case, her fingers found purchase on something—a necklace. It tore away from Barb's neck as Millie was tossed roughly away from the crowd.

"Barb, Barb; are you okay?" Millie rolled on the rough turf, feeling the dry stones scrape away her skin but not the shame that clung to her at that moment. The swarm of girls had descended on their leader who, while bruised and doubtlessly embarrassed, would not be seriously hurt.

"My necklace!" Barb exclaimed from within the crowd. Millie looked down in her hand, and sure enough, she was grasping the small steel chain, which contained a locket of some kind. Millie had pulled it from her victim's neck and still held it tight in her grip.

Millie leapt to her feet and held it high. "You want it? Come get it!" She took off, running way from the girls, from the safety of the compound, toward the fence.

Millie stumbled along as the ground grew even more treacherous and the terrain wilder. Since breaching the fence when she'd entered the compound last cycle, Millie hadn't been this close to it, but she was running on instinct now, fueled by sheer embarrassment, rage and fear. She could hear footsteps behind her. Doubtless, a few of the mindless drones had been dispatched to retrieve the prized possession of their leader.

Millie skidded to a halt a few meters from the fence, her calloused heels bitten by the now-completely rocky turf. She turned her head back to see that, as she suspected, two of the nearly identical followers of Barb were swiftly approaching.

Hoping that the girls were at least as interested in retrieving the locket as they were in smashing her face, Millie held the jewelry aloft, a rare stray bolt of sunlight glinting off the semi-tarnished surface.

"Stay right there or I swear to the One that I shall pitch this right over the fence." She hoped the girls wouldn't call her bluff, but her hope was in vain. They approached, their pristine faces contorting into what could only be described as sneers. "I'm not bluffing." But they knew she was, so as the got closer, Millie hesitated for only a split second, then turned and heaved with all her might, the locket sailing up and over the huge metal fence, into the Greyness beyond.

The girls were horrified.

One of them reared back to hit Millie, but the other grabbed the girl's arm and stopped her. She pointed at a petrified tree, long ago forgotten, that stood next to the fence, its stony branches stretching close to the top of the barrier.

The second girl lowered her arm and nodded to the first. Now it was Millie's turn to be horrified as the girls approached the tree, clearly considering going over the fence. Millie knew what it was like out there. She had lived it. She was certain that these girls had been born inside the compound and had only heard stories of the horrors.

Apparently, those stories weren't real enough to dissuade them from this foolish course.

"Wait! Don't!" Millie cried, stepping toward the tree, wishing the girls would listen to reason. "You don't know what could be out there. The Joyners…"

"Shut it, blobby!" one of the girls called out from the top branches of the stone tree. Millie winced at the insult, relieved that at least the monsters in her class hadn't chosen to play the tasteless and offensive game of Blob Tag. Not only did she cringe at the thought of touching the other girls as they joined together in the form of an amorphous blob attempting to swallow up all the other players, but the sheer idea of making fun and recreation out of tragedy was insulting and sickening.

Lost in thought, Millie barely noticed the girls drop over to the other side of the fence. She inhaled sharply. Even when the girls had reached the height of the tree, she hadn't believed they would go through with it. She figured they would take one look over the edge of the only world they had ever known, into the Greyness, the land of danger and despair on the other side, and their fear would get the best of them.

For an instant, Millie thought about going over the fence herself, going after them, rescuing them and the locket; being a hero and being accepted by Barb and the rest. But as she hesitated, she heard something that shook her bones.

It was a noise she had heard before, a terrifying, soul-rending sound that ran chilled daggers into her spinal column and wracked Millie to her very core.

It was cold, wet slurping, a bone-rending crunch, a choked gasp and a rhythmic, slapping, moving upward along the fence. Getting closer.

Slap, squish, slap, squish.

The terror rolled through Millie's body, locking her in place as if she had been frozen solid, just as her father had been all those years ago. But this was merely fear, not cryonic suspension. She could shake it off.

As she did, the slapping noise grew into an incessant pounding followed by a gradual cracking,

Slap, crack, slap, crack. CRASH!

The fence had been breached.

She ran.

Her feet were raw and bleeding by the time she arrived back at the play site. The girls had, in her absence, shifted their game to Blob Tag. In light of the events that were occurring behind her, Millie found it both tasteless and disturbing.

Barb was, of course, at the center of the blob. She was first to be it, and one by one, she had tagged the other girls, absorbing them into the massive blob-like structure that was growing, assimilating the masses of faceless toadies. It was a twisted perversion of the greatest threat that lay beyond the fence—a threat that was closing in.

"It's Mildred! Get her!" Barb yelled.

Millie stood in place, horrified, the mass of girls barreling down on her, as her mind envisioned the perversion of nature behind her, approaching faster than ever. She waved her arms, trying to shout down the horde, but they kept moving.

Then they stopped, frozen in place by what they saw behind Millie.

As the girls fell silent in awe, Millie heard the approaching sound.

Slap. Squish. Crunch.

Then a garbled cry of, "Help!"

Millie could see the faces of the girls, each converted into a rictus of pain and disgust; they were unable to move, but Millie, having been this close to the Joyners before, was not immobilized. She ran, pushing her way through the crowd, stumbling down the hill, skidding along the rocks as they ripped into her legs. She wondered, for a moment, if the blood would attract the creature. But then again, she figured it would be quite busy feasting on the helpless girls in front of it. Then, afterward, it would be stronger than ever, and who knew if it could be stopped.

She choked back a cry as she heard the first scream, followed by a squish, crunch and a wet slurping noise, then came the weeping and wailing.

Once more, Millie ran.

The screams and the slurping noises trailed behind Millie as she fled the scene. She wasn't sure if the sounds were growing louder as the creature grew in strength or if she was merely hearing the echoes of the fear and perversion of life that echoed in her memory. Either way, her stomach was bottoming out. If she'd eaten any solid food in the last light cycle, she would have vomited it up on the side of the path.

But she couldn't—she mustn't—stop running.

The creature was relentless, and the larger it grew, the faster it moved. She needed to put some distance between herself and it.

She needed to warn everyone else in the compound. She needed to find her mother and flee.

A rumble shook the ground beneath her. If the creature was done feasting, if its mass had grown… no, she stopped herself. It must be thunder of an approaching storm. Living inside the fence had softened her. Out in the Greyness, she had lived with the near-constant crash of thunder and lightning ripping across the night sky. That's what it was, she told herself, because the alternative, even considering her intense dislike of the girls, was too sickening to imagine.

As she approached the compound, she saw the first human she had encountered since leaving the girls. It was a boy she recognized, though barely. She had been segregated from the boys since she'd arrived, which was not a problem for her, having only seen her first male other than her father only a few cycles earlier; she couldn't say for sure who this boy was—they all looked the same to her, much like the girls as a matter of fact. He was square in the path of the oncoming creature and that put him in grave danger.

She waved her arms frantically, screaming until her throat was hoarse. As she neared, he finally looked up from his task—he seemed to be collecting rocks, no doubt for the ritual stoning scheduled for the next day. He flashed her a small smile and saluted, the customary greeting for a stranger.

"You need to run… Keith." She remembered his name, finally.

"What are you…" he started to ask, but then he felt the ground shudder. Looking past Millie, he caught sight of the oncoming shape, and she could see his jaw drop in astonishment. "What is that?"

She finally reached him and grabbed him by the arms. "You know exactly what it is, and you know we have to get out of here. We have to warn the others in the compound; we have to find the light."

He shook his head. "No. Not the compound. I don't think it's…" Knowing what it was now, he said the word with the gravitas it warranted, "…Heading there. Look."

Millie turned, gazing back at the top of the hill where she saw another figure, a second boy, walking toward them, dragging a sled of rocks behind him. She recognized him as one of the slower boys in the compound, someone she'd met only once; a child who had been relegated to manual labor due to his simpler mental faculties. He stood and waved, seemingly unaware of the monster looming behind him.

As Millie and Keith stood motionless, trapped in awe, they saw an ashen gray pseudopod arc up and over the top of the hillside, its surface undulating and pulsing. Millie was momentarily grateful that she wasn't closer, and therefore unable to see the twisted surface of the fleshy projection, for what she knew there was madness in it that she would never be able to *unsee*.

The pseudopod snaked out, snatching the unsuspecting boy by the waist, hoisting him high into the air, crushing his lungs so he couldn't even exhale, never mind scream. But Millie and Keith could hear another sound, one far more disturbing. It was the wet, sloppy squish of absorption, of the loss of identity and assimilation into the massive, twisted gestalt of flesh and bone, of mindlessness and predatory hunger.

When Millie heard a whimper, she was unsure if it was the boy's or her own. She supposed it didn't matter. She could just make out the hazy, amorphous shape of the Joyner, traveling the way the boy had come, moving away from the compound, following the path the poor child had just trod.

"Come on!" Keith called out, grabbing Millie by the arm and tugging her out of her shock. "We need to get to the quarry. That's where there's the most people."

Her legs finally responded to his pull and she fell in step beside him. "But what can we do once we get there?" she asked.

He tried to shrug as he ran, his bare feet slapping on the sandy ground. "Warn them. Plus, if they have their survival kits, they should have a portable light with them. Maybe, if we can get there before it gets much bigger, that'll be enough."

She knew that was a big maybe.

The one fact she knew for sure about the creature is that it was slow and plodding. At least at its smaller sizes. The more it absorbed, the faster it became. Millie said a silent prayer to the One that she and Keith would make it to the quarry in time to warn the others. She didn't know the route, of course, being new to the compound, but she followed Keith, trusting that he knew the shortest path.

They crested a ridge and suddenly they were looking down on the quarry.

The men of the compound milled about, extracting stone from the earth, stone bound for reinforcing and growing the fence, for protecting the compound. Millie knew they would need that stone to rebuild the section of the fence the creature had ruined and she fervently hoped that these men would be able to protect themselves from it.

As she gazed down, though, she saw the first heartening sight of the day: one man, worn and haggard, perhaps even as old as thirty-five years, held a small tube which glowed with light. He was using it, she supposed, to carve the stone itself, but she knew it had other uses, and she hoped it had the power to strike back and defeat the Joyner.

She and Keith ran down the hill, yelling, one on top of the other.

The old man—Jake was the name on his jumpsuit—stopped cutting and put up a hand, a bemused grimace forming on his face. "Slow down. Just what in the name of the One are you going on about?"

Keith and Millie looked at one another. Keith nodded slightly and she took a deep breath.

"It's a Joyner," Millie said, quietly but firmly. There was no point dancing around the details. There was simply no time. To his credit, Jake asked no questions. Perhaps he could see the genuine fear in Millie's eyes. Perhaps he knew of her story and her experience out in the Greyness. Perhaps he was just wise enough to take such a statement seriously on its face value and deal with the consequences later. He hoisted the light weapon onto his shoulder. "Where?" he said.

Millie turned, ready to point in the direction of the approaching creature, but she was too late. It was already there. The cacophonous sounds of the quarry had masked its approach, and now it was too late.

The first indication of its arrival was a pair of tendrils shooting over the lip of the quarry and down on the unsuspecting workers. Keith was seeing the phenomenon up close for the first time and he dropped to one knee, retching violently.

She didn't blame him.

The smell itself was enough to induce vomiting. It didn't so much as waft across the quarry as assault the senses, punching one in the nose with its foul stench. If she'd been pressed to categorize the odor, she would have described it as a mix of decayed and rotting flesh, oozing feces and sweat, tinged with a salty dash of tears and the coppery tang of blood.

But the smell was only part of the horror. The rending, squishing noise ripped through the air, drowning out the metallic clang of the equipment. But the sight, well, that was the image that had haunted Millie's dreams for the better part of her childhood, that had ruined many a night's sleep with sweat and screams and tears. As much as she'd despised the girls who'd been taunting her earlier that day, she'd never have wished a fate like this on them, or anyone.

She swore she could make out some of their faces, warped and flowing, the agony written large in their eyes as their features shifted and moved across the surface of the tendril. But the faces weren't all she could see in the body of the creature.

The tendrils were in constant motion. A mottle of skin colors ran and swirled along the surface as bones and joints rose and fell along the edges of the snaky protrusion. As the body parts of the absorbed victims shifted and moved, their screams and wails could be heard as their mouths came and went.

Then the tendrils wrapped around the first two workers, absorbing them into the creature's mass, their cries were added to the disharmonious mix. With a sickening slurping noise, the two workers lost their identities for good, their beings now irrevocably a part of the creature. Their flesh melted into the pseudopod, their bones crunching, their skin splaying and flaying into the mass of amalgamated body parts. It was over in a matter of seconds, and the increase in mass only served to jumpstart the Joyner.

It flowed over the crest of the quarry in its full and terrible glory.

The body of the Joyner, such as it was, consisted of the absorbed victims, their mass, their flesh and their ever-shifting parts. The faces and limbs of the girls that had tormented Millie earlier that day erupted on the surface of the creature, screaming and flailing, then receding back into the mass of ever-shifting flesh with whimpers and splattering sounds.

Millie grabbed Keith, still clearly shaken from the sight, and pulled him toward the edge of the quarry. As they fled, the creature made short work of the rest of the men, the high-pitched shrieks of the girls that made up the mindless beast now mingled with deeper moans of agony from the men who had fought valiantly but fruitlessly, trying to hold onto their sense of self, their very bodies.

But it was hopeless.

In a matter of moments, the Joyner had nearly doubled in size, swallowing up the men, joining their mass into the collective, the creature adding rippling muscle and shocks of wild hair to its lithe form.

Keith was on the verge of tears, watching the men he had known all his life devoured by the soulless monstrosity. Millie gripped his arm, trying to choke back her own sobs.

Through her tears, she could see Jake, gripping the light projector and stepping forward with an enormous yell of desperation and fury. It sprung to life and hummed, a bright luminescence erupting from the maw of the weapon, blasting into the creature.

Where it struck the surface of the Joyner, its flesh seared and smoked, a horrific stench roiling off the scorched skin. The faces melting to and fro contorted in agony, shrill cries of pain ripping through the air.

As the creature shifted and changed, the scorch marks healed, and Jake continued to pour on the heat, shouting louder and louder as the Joyner moved closer and closer.

Then, with a quick strike and a sickening squish, Jake, as an individual, was no more.

He had been absorbed. At that moment, Keith and Millie gripped each other tight. They had nowhere left to run, and with the current size and speed of the creature, no hope of fleeing.

The Joyner moaned and wailed, the faces and forms shifting and rippling as it drew toward them.

Millie held her breath, thinking of her mother, and wondering if her mom would be able to escape, to find a new life, to start over. She opened her eyes, staring right into the agonized visage of Barb, as her former nemesis' sad face crawled across the surface of the creature.

Keith was quickly grabbed and pulled from her grasp, his screams filling her ears.

Then the mass of flesh lurched forward again, engulfing Millie in its warmth and wetness, absorbing her flesh into the collective, and taking away her individuality forever.

SAVAGE NEW WORLD

ANTHONY GIANGREGORIO

Twenty years after World War 3, the planet is a very different place. The land has been decimated from both nuclear and biological missiles. The United States is nothing but a burnt-out shell, a decayed husk where the few remaining humans struggle to eke out a pitiful existence.

Many parts of the country are still radioactive and are impassible. The world has thirty percent less oxygen and the sky is covered in purple and green clouds that threaten to drop acid rain at any second.

Where the land was once stable, now it is constantly torn asunder by chasms, landslides, earthquakes—and in the colder areas—avalanches. Mutated animals of all kinds roam the countryside, each more horrible to behold than the last. Killer dogs and rats of equal size are among the worst. Traveling in packs, they will devour anything unfortunate enough to cross their path. Lizards have transformed into dragon-like creatures and insects are now as large as a man's head, while spiders can grow up to six feet wide and five feet high. Genetic mutations run amuck, with no end in sight.

It is a bleak time to be alive, but despite this, there are some who refuse to bow down to nature gone mad. In a world where the gun is king and a sharp blade is queen, some make their way across the blighted landscape, selling their gun-hands for quick cash or a bed for the night.

Even in this dark place, there are settlements scattered across the land, where likeminded individuals are struggling to scratch a living from the barren soil.

High in the mountains, the rain began to pour, the green and purple clouds releasing their payload by the millions of gallons. With the land all but scrub and dirt, a flash flood was inevitable. Dry earth soon became mud as the onslaught of water rolled down the mountains and into the low prairie land.

By the time the mudslide had reached sea level, it was twenty-five feet of liquid death and still growing; filled with the detritus of life, now all dead.

Rolling across the prairie, the massive wave absorbed every-thing it came across, sucking it into the dark sea of death.

Parched wastelands that hadn't seen water in years were sud-denly inundated as the giant wave moved across the land. Within its maw, drowned animals bobbed about, old cars, bits of houses, and uprooted trees. The wave was more than a half mile wide and still becoming wider. Nothing could escape its power.

Propelled like lava from an active volcano, the wave pushed across the blighted land, leaving nothing but drowned carcasses in its wake as the water level rose steeply.

It was death personified, and nothing living would escape its clutches.

Martin Steele held up his right arm, his hand closed into a fist to warn the others to stop walking. At thirty-eight years of age, he was a tall man, topping over six feet, with skin as tan and dark as the metal of the gun he carried—a S&W .357 Magnum. The power-ful gun was in a shoulder holster and a sawed-off shotgun was strapped to his hip, as well as a ten inch hunting knife. A bandolier hung over his shoulder, filled with shells for the room sweeper. Though not a good weapon for long distance, the shotgun could take down anything before it if the confines were close enough.

Behind Steele were his two traveling companions. The first was a beautiful woman in her late thirties with full breasts and thin hips. Her lips were naturally red, her cheeks always holding a blush. She was pretty in a way that modern civilization hadn't appreciated. Though not wearing makeup, her hair wild and untamed, and needing to be brushed desperately, she carried with her a sexuality that would make any man kill to bed her. Not that it would matter. She belonged to Steele, the two being lovers for over three years and counting.

Though her full name was Kimberly, she went simply by Kim, and though she had a last name, she almost never used it, as there was no need—not anymore. She cared a semi-auto .45 pistol with a fifteen round clip and a six inch hunting knife, one weapon on each hip. A camo-colored backpack was slung over her shoulder, filled with supplies and spare ammunition.

She stopped walking at his warning and studied Steele's back, at his powerful shoulders and strong legs. When the two made love, it was like wild animals were battling for dominance. Scratches and bites were commonplace and both partners would always end up exhausted, their lovemaking so passionate that time seemed to stand still.

The last in the group was an older man in his late fifties. He carried a cane to help him walk and a large backpack was on his shoulders. Though food and water were something beyond precious, the old man carried more books than supplies. He had been a professor many years ago, before the bombs fell, and though the world had no need for scholars, he refused to entirely turn his back on the old ways. But he wasn't a fool either and so had embraced the new ways of the world as well. On his hip was a .357 Colt Python, the large handgun making his pants drop slightly from its weight. He would constantly have to hitch them up or else risk stepping on his pant legs. He wore a faded tan frock coat and a fedora to keep the sun off his balding pate. A pair of wire-rimmed glasses rode his aristocratic nose, the spectacles cherished more than everything else he owned. If he broke them, there would be no replacement, and without them he was blind as a bat. His full name was Theodore Algernon Damascus, though Steele and Kim simple called him Prof, which was short for Professor. Whether the title was one that pleased the older man had never been broached. Back when Steele had saved the professor from a horde of blood-thirsty cannibals, the last thing on the professor's mind was to contradict Steele after introducing himself. If Steele hadn't come along, he would have ended up being the dinner special that night. Steele had cut a bloody swath through the cannibals and come out whole on the other side, and left in his path had been nothing but bloody bodies. The two men had become fast friends that day, and Steele had once confided in the professor that he thought of the older man as a father figure.

The professor stopped next to Kim as Steele cocked his head to the side, then lowered his arm.

"What's wrong?" Kim asked, her hand going to her .45, her fingers caressing the grip.

"You don't hear that?" he asked. "It's like a rumbling. It reminds me of when I was a boy and I used to feel the train tracks when the train was coming."

She slowed her breathing and strained to hear, and then yes, she could hear it, too. It reminded her of the sound horses made when a herd was galloping, only it was faint, just on the edge of her hearing level. In the middle of the barren plain the three were on, the idea of a herd of horses was ludicrous and so was quickly dismissed.

Suddenly, from some dense brush a few feet away, the sounds of scrambling could be heard, as if from many creatures. All three turned and reached for their weapons, assuming they were under attack from God knew what.

A giant moose appeared, its body gaunt from lack of food. Behind it were dogs, rats, a few deer, a family of coyote, and other animals that should normally be natural enemies and never in any sane world would they travel together without attacking one another.

The moose was coming directly at the three companions and Steele and the others braced for the assault. Steele lined up the head of the moose in his gun sight, and was about to pull the trigger, when the moose veered to the side and continued running, as did the rest of the animals.

The three humans stood in amazement as the crowd of animals swerved around them and charged across the land without so much as a glance at the three humans standing in their midst.

In seconds, the herd of animals had gone by and only the trampled brush and other hardy foliage, now flattened into a green muck, remained. Seconds later, more animals appeared, though these were stragglers and trailed behind the main herd of animals.

"What the hell was that all about?" Kim asked as she stared at the backs of the fleeing animals. It wasn't long before they were lost in a cloud of dust.

Steele shook his head. "Don't know." He sniffed, trying to pick up the odor of a wildfire, but all he detected was the stench of the animals' feces when they let fly as they ran. "But something sure has spooked the wildlife."

"Perhaps it would be a good idea if we joined them until we know what's going on," the professor suggested.

Steele didn't have to be told twice. "Damn good idea, Prof. Let's move out, and double time it."

With Steele in the lead, they began to run, following the wide path the animals had made. As they ran, more animals joined them from all sides, and all had eyes wide with fear. None of the animals acknowledged the humans, all focused on running away from something.

Steele noticed the professor was lagging behind, the weight of his backpack full of books slowing him down. "Maybe you should leave the books, Prof," he suggested. "You can come back and get them later, once whatever danger is freaking out the animals had passed."

"Not on you life, Martin," the professor huffed. "These books are worth more to me than my life. I shalt not let them be lost forever. Lord knows this world has fallen into depravity as it is. I will not let it sink even more into the depths of Hell."

"Whatever," Steele said simply, knowing to argue with the older man would be a waste of time. "Just keep up."

The three travelers slowed to a steady jog to conserve energy, as more animals passed them as if the trio were standing still. Steele could have run three times as fast as the professor and double that of Kim, but he held back, wanting to stay with his friends.

A mile into the dash to escape the unknown danger, Steele took the pack full of books from the professor, realizing the older man was about to collapse with fatigue. Though Steele's arms were heavily muscled, his shoulders wide, even he felt the weight of the books and grudgingly gave the professor a nod of respect for carrying the leaded weight.

"What do you think it is if it's not a wildfire?" Kim asked as she jogged next to Steele. Her ample breasts rose and fell gracefully and he had a hard time looking away.

"No idea, but we need to find out. For all we know the danger's passed and we're running for nothing."

"Mayhap I might offer a suggestion, dear Martin," the professor said.

"I'm all ears, Prof," Steele replied.

The professor pointed to a copse of dead trees a hundred yards in the distance, though off to the right, meaning they would have to detour from the trodden path of the fleeing animals. After the first mile, the amount of wildlife had dwindled to only a few. Though barren of leaves, the tree trunks were majestic, signifying that the trees had to be over a hundred years old. "Perhaps you could climb one of those large fellows and see if our back trail is clear."

Steele grinned. "That's a damn good idea, Prof. Sounds like a plan."

The trio peeled off the path and began running for the trees. As they ran, the clouds in the sky began to rumble. A storm was coming, which was never a good thing.

They reached the treeline in a short amount of time, and after dropping the pack of books to the ground, Steele shimmied up a tree with a trunk as thick as four men pressed together in a circle. As he climbed, his fingers search for crevices in the bark and more than a few times the bark gave way, now dry and brittle from lack of water. Like a monkey, he scaled the trunk and was soon halfway up the giant tree.

"How're you doing?" Kim called up. Her head was tilted back, her left hand over her eyes to block out the sunlight, her hair blowing behind her like a halo. To Steele she had never looked more beautiful.

"So far so good," he said and grabbed a tree limb and hauled himself up another two feet. It was as he placed his foot on the limb that a dry crack filled the air and he found himself falling. His stomach flipped upside down as the sense of gravity he had come to take for granted was lost. As his body began to plummet, his arms snapped out and his hands grabbed anything they could come in contact with. The first branch he grabbed simply broke off as well, but the next one was more stable and he found his body halted, the tug on his arms from his own weight enough to make him wince.

Below, both Kim and the professor cried out as they jumped to the side to avoid the falling limb.

"Martin, are you okay?" Kim called up to him.

"Yeah, I'm fine. Just gotta pay more attention." With his heart beating a steady staccato in his chest, he dry swallowed and continued the climb, taking even more care than he had before. If he fell and broke a bone, there would be no hospital to go to, no on-call doctors waiting to treat him.

Minutes later, he finally reached the top, or as close to the top as he dared. This high, the top swayed with the wind, and he felt his stomach drop each time the tip of the tree bowed to the side, to then slowly return to its original position.

Pushing his sawed-off to the side, he reached down and un-zipped a small black pouch attached to his waist. He slid a hand into the pouch and pulled out a tiny pair of binoculars. The binocs were barely four inches wide but they were in perfect working order and were powerful.

Raising them to his eyes, he peered off into the distance behind him, his imagination trying to tell him what he would see before he did. As his eyes went wide, he refocused the binocs, not able to believe what he was seeing.

There it was in all its horrible glory.

It looked like the side of a mountain—a moving mountain.

Dark brown and black in some places, the wall of water resembled mud more than water. As he studied the wall, he could see the poor creatures that hadn't been fast enough to escape and had been taken into the rush of liquid death to then drown.

Steele turned around in the tree to see what was before him on the horizon, searching for an incline, a mountain, an old building, anything tall enough that it could be used to climb and escape the wall of death.

High in the tree, without any obstacles to slow or dampen sound, the onslaught of the massive wave came to Steele's ears. The power of millions of gallons of water, and more growing every minute, came to him as the rushing tide spilled across the barren earth.

Steele tried to stay calm, to remain focused, for to panic would be instant death. His eyes searched the horizon some more, his mouth moving as he sent up a few prayers to whatever god was interested in hearing them at the moment. Then he saw it, off to the left of his current position, about two miles off, give or take.

It looked like a small hill, oddly shaped but still, it was high land…and the only place worth trying for. Quickly putting the binoculars away and not bothering to zip the pouch, he began to climb down the tree. He moved fast, barely holding on as he went from limb to limb. More than once he almost fell, but he shrugged it off and continued moving.

Now more than ever, time was the enemy.

When he was no more than ten feet off the ground, he let go and fell, landing heavily, his powerful legs taking the impact as he bent them.

"What did you see?" Kim asked when she saw Steele's hardened visage. She and the professor had been hiding behind the tree so as not be trampled by all the animals constantly flowing past them as more arrived and spread out, running off in all directions.

"Something impossible," Steele said simply.

"What does that mean, dear boy? Explain further, please," the professor said as he shifted from foot to foot.

Steele frowned deeply. "There's some kind of massive tidal wave coming right for us. It's maybe five miles away but it's moving fast. We need to get to high ground or we're done for."

Both Kim and the professor turned to where they'd come from, trying to see the tidal wave Steele spoke of. Neither could see anything.

"You can't see it from here," Steele said. "It's too far away. But trust me, it's moving fast. Come, on, I saw a hill two miles away or so. If we double-time it, we just might make it before we're drowned."

Both Kim and the professor knew not to argue. If Steele said a massive wall of water was heading right for them, they knew it was the truth, and the fleeing animals only added to the truthfulness of the tale.

Gathering their meager supplies, the trio began to run in the direction Steele had directed, joining more escaping animals. Bumped from all sides, the companions had to fight to stay upright as the frightened animals snorted and howled in fear.

One time the professor let out a yelp and began to fall after tripping on a large rat, but Steele was able to grab him and keep him upright before he fell. A good thing too, as the animals would have simply trampled over him, crushing his body into the denuded ground.

"Thank you, Martin, that was a close one," the professor said, his breathing ragged.

"Keep up, Prof, you're slowing us down. We need to move faster."

"Then you must go on without me, dear boy. I fear I am at the end of my rope. Go, I'll be right behind you," he said valorously.

"No can do, Prof," Steele replied. "We all get there in one piece or none of us do." He reached under the professor's shoulders and picked the man up, then swung him over his left shoulder.

"Martin, what are you doing? Put me down this instant!"

"Not gonna happen, Prof, now just be still and let me do the work."

The professor looked like he was going to protest further but then he went limp, knowing once Steele had his mind made up there would be no talking him out of it. The two men had that in common if anything.

The trio began running again, Steele with the professor on one shoulder and the older man's pack full of books on the other. Kim followed close behind, doing her best to keep the animals from coming too close and getting in Steele's way.

Soon, a mile was under their feet, but the next one was the hardest. The animals had thinned out now, most running ahead of the three humans. The land gave way to nothing but bushland, weeds and low shrubs, which was the only foliage dotting the otherwise barren landscape.

Kim had her mouth open, her breath ragged as she ran by Steele's side. Though made of iron, even Steele was becoming exhausted. Not that it was anything to be ashamed of. With over two hundred pounds of weight on his back, only his iron will kept him going.

Minutes passed in silence, only the couple's crunching footsteps breaking the quiet.

Then another sound began to be heard, and though faint, it was a portent of things to come. The sound of millions of gallons of rushing water.

But the hill was now in sight, the one that Steele had spied with his binoculars when in the tree. As the couple ran for their lives, the hill began to grow bigger, and it gave them all the motivation to run faster, though both were exhausted.

"Put me down, Martin, I can go the rest of the way on my own locomotion," the professor spit as he kicked his feet like a petulant child.

Not wanting to argue and too tired to do so even if he wanted to, Steele let the older man drop to the ground, where the professor picked himself up with a few muffled curses. Steele felt like the weight of the world had been lifted from him and the pack with the books felt as if it weighed a mere pound.

It spurred him on with renewed energy, and after slipping an arm under Kim's shoulder, he half-carried her as the three made a dash for the hill.

The roaring of water was louder as well, and when Steele looked down, he saw that the ground was wet with an inch of water and was slowly rising with each passing second.

"Faster, we're almost there," he said and began to run harder, pretty much carrying Kim.

Then they reached the hill, which was steeper than any of them could have imagined from when seeing it in the distance. A few animals had tried to climb it but had failed miserably, only the nimblest able to make it to the top.

Steele saw there were vents sticking out of the hill on all sides, and unknown to him, it had been the site of a garbage dump at one time, and when it had been filled, it was covered with soil and forgotten. The vents were there to allow methane to escape as the garbage rotted within the mountain of trash.

Dropping the pack of books and feeling quite the fool for still carrying them, Steele pulled out his binoculars and peered at his back tail.

The wall of water nearly took up the entire lens and stretched from side to side so that there was no relief. Now that the wave was closer, he could make out the detritus within it in even more detail. There was a dented and twisted eighteen wheeler, the tires gone and the windows shattered, a few more wrecked cars, trees uprooted, and more animal carcasses than he could count even if he had the time. The wall of death could now be seen by the naked eye as it flowed across the land, sweeping up any animals too slow to escape its clutches. It was still miles away but closing fast, and on top of the oncoming wave, the water level had been slowly growing so that Steele's ankles were now covered.

Under his feet, the ground shook as the death wave continued ever onward.

He let everyone rest for a full thirty seconds, knowing he needed it as bad as both Kim and the professor.

"Let's start climbing, I'll take lead," he said simply, and withdrew his ten-inch hunting knife. He cut a piece of rope taken from Kim's backpack and quickly tied it around the professor, then he picked up the pack of books and slung it over his shoulder again. He winced as the weight bore down on him. He stabbed the knife into the side of the hill, then began to pull himself up.

His feet found purchase immediately and he slowly began to scale the hill. When he was ten feet off the ground, he felt the rope go taut and then ease up as the professor began to climb, using the holes Steele had made with the knife.

Kim followed next, her agility making the climb child's play for her.

For Steele in the lead, who had to make the handholds, it wasn't an easy climb due to the angle of the hill. It was almost completely vertical, and only his powerful arms and legs kept him from falling, both trembling from the exertion before he was halfway up.

But that was a good thing in its own way. The hill looked like it would be high enough to protect them from the tidal wave, the odds that the water would rise over forty feet doubtful.

With each passing yard of distance taken, the wave was diminishing in size, its energy becoming spent, though it had been so massive to start out that even after a dozen miles it still had power.

Steele finally made it to the top of the hill, and as he tried to clamber over the edge, he found it was more difficult than it should have been. The top of the hill was covered in sand, and each time he tried to sink his knife into it to pull himself over the edge, the knife simply slid back to him, leaving a thin line in the sand. He couldn't get a foothold.

"Prof, I need you to give me a push!" Steele called down over his shoulder.

"Whatever I can do to help, Martin, just say when," the professor replied.

Steele reached out with the knife yet again and stabbed the sand, then yelled, "Now, Prof!" as he strained his arms and shoulders, hauling himself up. He let out a groan of fury as he used all his remaining strength to pull himself up and over.

At first he didn't move, but then he felt the professor's hands on his butt and though the effort was weak, it was just enough to give Steele the boost he needed.

First one hand got some traction and then the other, and a second later he had a leg over. He rolled onto the sandy top of the hill, he gazed up at the colored clouds, for just one second wanting to rest, to even close his eyes and sleep. His shotgun dug into his back as he lay on it but he didn't care, just glad to rest his weary limbs.

"Ah, hello there! Martin? A little help, please!" the professor's voice called from over the edge.

"Shit," Steele whispered; he'd forgotten his teammates.

Rolling to the side, he grabbed the rope still attached to him and began to pull on it. The professor, not weighing much, was easy to get over the edge and onto the sandy soil, and one arm at a time, the man was soon off to the side and on solid ground. Kim was next, and though sand was kicked into each other's faces as she was pulled onto the top of the hill, soon she was lying beside Steele, her chest heaving from the climb, her mouth tight as she sucked in air through her nose.

Now that he had a moment to rest, Steele stood up slowly and had a look around the plateau the group was on. The instant his eyes scanned over the area, he didn't like what he saw, not by a longshot.

The entire center of the plateau was filled with animals, those that had been nimble enough to make the climb up the steep incline on one of the four sides. The odd thing was that the animals packed together were both hunter and prey, just like the escaping herds, but at the moment none were attacking one another. For this one moment in time, the fear of the rushing wave of water was enough to override their natural instincts to kill one another. Natural enemies now stood side by side, huddled on the top of the mesa as they waited for the passing of the tidal wave. They were packed in tight, however, and every few seconds one would end up too close to the edge and tumble off, usually followed by a terrified bleating, howl or snarl.

Shrubs and even a few small trees dotted the area, though even the animals that ate shrubbery ignored them, all too frightened to even think of eating.

As Steele's eyes studied the assortment of wildlife trapped on the plateau with him and his friends, his eyes went to a section in the middle of the creatures, a section that was all but empty, with the exception of one creature in the exact center.

About fifty feet away from Steele, standing over ten feet tall on its hind legs, was something only once imagined in horror movies. It mostly resembled a lizard, with its dark green scales and flickering tongue. But that was where the resemblance stopped. It stood on four legs normally, but had the ability to pop up on its rear legs and actually walk like a man. Steele's first thoughts were that it reminded him of a Gila monster, right down to the scales, only a hundred times larger than its namesake. Its eyes were a dark red and seemed to glow.

At the moment, none of that mattered. All that did was Steele didn't like being on the hill with the mutant and neither did the lizard. As if on cue, it stood up on its hind legs and hissed at Steele, Kim and the professor, then began to approach.

As it moved closer, Steele saw its face better and he grimaced. The snout was elongated, like an alligator, and it had three rows of serrated teeth, each row sharper than the former, the smallest as long as six inches, and all were curved inward inside the powerful jaws. The creature looked as if it could snap Steele in half with no effort.

As it came forward, its front claws flexed, as if the creature was already imagining tearing the three humans apart. Its red eyes went wider, as if molten lava flowed within its head.

"Kim, stay with Prof. I'll distract it," Steele said and shifted to the left, where there was little room to maneuver. "If it tries for you, shoot it, but otherwise leave it to me."

"Be careful, it looks like a mean bastard," she said, drawing her .45 but holding fire.

"Don't let it bite you, Martin!" the professor called out, also seeing the similarity of the creature to a Gila monster. "If it's like a regular Gila then its bite is poisonous, but only if it's able to get you in a certain pose and then only if it begins to masticate you."

Steele grinned slightly at the professor's warning. If the lizard did bite him, no doubt it would take the limb clean off, let alone get to chew on it. "Will do, Prof, that's good to know. Thanks for the advice," he said simply as he unslung his sawed-off from off his shoulder. Though the weapon was powerful, he knew it would take more than a few blasts to take this beast down. The monster's scales looked like hammered iron, with not so much as an inch open that might be considered a weak spot.

Its forked tongue flicked out, tasting the air, as it hissed and roared at the same time. Steele saw that its muzzle and nostrils were covered in dried blood. The mutant had fed recently, and no doubt had been disturbed by the approaching tidal wave. But now that it was on the hill and felt safe, its stomach was rumbling again and it was time to feed once more. Unfortunately for Steele and his friends, the mutant preferred human meat over any other prey.

"Hey, ugly, over here!" Steele yelled to get the mutant lizard's attention. Though it worked, deep down he kind of wished it hadn't. Now the creature only had eyes for him. It dropped down on all fours and lowered its head, its back legs flexing, its rump slowly rising into the air. Steele recognized the posture—it was going to charge him.

"Careful, Martin, it looks like it's going to attack," the professor called, seeing the action of the mutant as well.

Steele didn't reply, too focused on the enemy before him. He leveled the sawed-off but didn't shoot—not yet. For the maximum amount of damage, he needed to let the lizard get closer, and even then it was risky.

His eyes scanned the creature once more, trying to find a weak spot. Then, his gaze went to the giant lizard's throat as it swallowed. He watched the flesh beneath the scales undulate and realized that the scales were spaced father apart there. Made sense. It would need to be flexible in the throat area, as the creature needed to swallow its kills, taking down the large chunks of meat after it ripped its prey apart with its rows of teeth.

And then the lizard began to run, its head almost touching the ground to protect its vulnerable area, its powerful legs, each the size of Steele's waist, stomping into the sand and spraying it in all directions.

As it came for him, Steele decided on a different tactic—he needed help. "Prof, Kim, shoot the damn thing! Fire at will! Distract it from me so I can get a shot at its neck! " He squeezed the trigger of the shotgun and rolled out of the way of the attacking mutant. The buckshot hit the beast square in the face, but the giant lizard closed its red eyes before any serious damage could be done. Steele saw that all he'd done was piss it off even more, if that was even possible.

From the side, fifteen feet away, the professor and Kim began to fire at the mutant. The other animals, terrified of the gunshots, tried to back up even further to the edge of the plateau, some falling off to land in still heaps on the ground from broken necks. The water level was rising as well and the carcasses became half-submerged. The sound of rushing water was growing louder also, as the tidal wave grew ever closer.

The first bullet fired by the professor struck the mutant just behind its front leg. He saw it hit and also watched it rebound off the steel-like scales. However, the creature let out a roar of pain and spun about to face what it realized was an attack from more than one side. Kim took this opportunity to line up a shot with the lizard's face, preferably its left eye. As the beast spun to face her and the professor, she sent a high velocity round that traveled four hundred and eighty feet per second. Her maximum distance would have been two hundred and forty yards, so she was well in her killing radius. The bullet flew true and entered the left eye, pulping it and sending pinkish ooze squirting out of the orbital socket. Unfortunately, though the bullet shattered the eye, it didn't continue into the brain, but instead rebounded off the ocular socket to then exit just above the eye. Though blinded in one eye and angry, the mutant was still very active.

Steele fired another burst from his sawed-off, striking the creature in the side of the head. It roared again, trying to decide which attacker to go at first. Steele solved the problem by shooting again, the buckshot peppering the lizard's face and some stray shot going into the ruined eye. More pain filled the mutant's head and it hissed and roared, its tongue lashing out at empty air.

The mutant turned and charged at Steele, the warrior doing the same. At the last second, before the two would have collided, Steele lunged to the side but leveled his shotgun at the lizard's throat. He fired at the exact moment he flew past the mutant and the buckshot exploded out of the chopped-down barrel and struck the creature dead on in the throat.

Thinking victory was his, Steele was shocked when he felt something wrap around his right ankle and whip him about like a rag doll. The lizard's tail? He'd forgotten about it. The mutant was more agile than Steele ever would have believed. As soon as he was knocked to the dirt, the tail retracted. Steele rolled over as soon as he landed, afraid the mutant was about to pounce on him and tear his body to shreds. With the claws the beast had it would be easy for it to do. Steele's only hope was luck and his speed. Though the mutant was fast, Steele was still the more agile of the two.

As he got to his feet, he found he needn't have worried, as the mutant was otherwise engaged. To let him gain his feet, both Kim and the professor were laying down covering fire, keeping the giant lizard focused on them. Steele saw blood on the mutant's throat where he'd shot it but it wasn't a killing shot. The throat might have been the weakest link on the beast's body, but it was still a hard nut to crack.

Then the tail whipped out again and wrapped around Kim's arm. Before she could do anything, the lizard pulled her to it and slammed her to the ground. She had just enough time to roll onto her back before the mutant's head snapped forward, and sank its teeth into her neck right below her chin, tearing out her throat in one massive bite, and nearly severing her head from her shoulders. More than half her throat was taken out with the brutal attack and she spit blood, bleeding out in seconds. Hot blood splashed onto the lizard's legs as it chewed the flesh within its mouth, relishing the hot taste of fresh human meat.

Blood gushed out of the gash that was once Kim's neck like a river, soaking into the ground as her arms and legs spasmed in death. The lizard snapped its head down again, slurping at the blood, satiating its hunger for the moment.

"Oh my God, no, Kim!" Steele screamed when he saw his lover go down. But he could already see it was too late to save her. Her eyes were open but saw nothing, her chest still. She was gone. It had happened so fast, so sudden, it seemed like it wasn't real. How could it be? After so many scrapes together, after so many battles, to then have her die in such a foolish way. It seemed such a waste. As warriors of the new world, both of them had accepted death as a way of life. But to die in battle was the way they had wanted to go, side by side as they took as many of their enemies with them as they could before succumbing to their wounds.

No, this wasn't right, it wasn't fair. She couldn't die like this. He wouldn't allow it.

Yet he knew no matter how much he ranted, it was for nothing. Death was the great equalizer, and no matter what a man might want, in the end, Death would call the shots, would make the final decision.

"You son-of-a-bitch," Steele hissed. "I'll fucking kill you!" Though his voice was hard, it was also calm. Walking forward, he let the sawed-off fall from his hands to hang on its lanyard. He pulled his .357 Magnum and held it before him with both hands, approaching the creature with purpose.

The mutant's head popped up and its remaining eye swiveled to see another human walking towards it. Excellent, another meal, it thought. Its small brain wondered why these humans died so easily, why they didn't run away like the other prey did. No matter, its stomach was still empty and more meat would be welcome.

Ignoring Kim's cooling corpse, the lizard jumped up and faced the oncoming prey, its tale flicking back and forth. The entire hill rumbled as the tidal wave came closer. It had only been a few minutes since Steele and his friends had reached the plateau, though it seemed like hours had passed.

A hissing roar left its mouth as the giant lizard began to charge Steele, its blood-coated muzzle catching the sun and glinting with gore. Steele didn't so much as flinch, his eyes creased, his jaw taut. This beast had to die. It was him or it, one would lay dead and bleeding when the next minute was over.

As the mutant came for him, Steele leveled the Magnum and began to fire. His arm was like his namesake and the muzzle of the gun didn't so much as waver a half inch before realigning on its target. The first bullet struck the lizard in the chest, and the second hit the exact same spot. The impact of both rounds knocked off one of the iron scales. Steele kept firing, his body like a statue. He wasn't moving from the spot he'd picked to make his stand. A line in the sand had been drawn, and that line had been drawn with blood—Kim's blood.

The third bullet hit a quarter of an inch off from the first two, but it was still close enough to penetrate the thick skin of the mutant. Dark blood began to spurt from the wound and the creature faltered in its charge, not understanding why it felt pain from within, yet nothing had attacked it.

The next round struck the lizard's stomach, which was lightly armored, and the next round struck its front right leg. The scales protected the leg but not enough from cracking bone. The mutant dropped to the ground, but regained its feet, though now it limped.

It had almost reached Steele. The warrior still didn't flinch, though the mutant lizard was far from dead. The beast roared in anger at the wounds it had suffered, its one red eye locked onto Steele, wanting nothing more than to tear the man apart.

It came forward again, a new intensity in its remaining eye.

Steele slowly bent his knees as he went into a crouch. He needed to be like this so he had the best vantage point for the shot he planned to take. As the lizard reached Steele and loomed over him, he raised the muzzle of the Magnum so that it was aimed directly at the lizard's throat—the weakest part of its anatomy.

He fired calmly as the mutant raised its head to strike, only his bullet was far faster than the beast could ever have imagined. The round tore straight up and caught the lizard just under its jaw, right where the scales of its chest met those on its throat. In this one spot, there was only its thick, leathery hide and though tough, it wasn't strong enough to stop a .357 caliber bullet.

The bullet entered the throat and tore out its windpipe, then ricocheted upward and into its brain. The round pulverized the brain before the lizard knew it was dead. But Steele didn't know this and he was already firing again. This bullet entered a few inches to the side of the last one, struck a row of teeth, pulverizing them, to then exit out the side of its face, taking the teeth with it. Like shrapnel, the teeth tore out half the face, black tendrils of gore and veins spraying out in all directions.

In its death throes, the mutant still fought, determined to take Steele with it into the black void of oblivion. It towered over the man and then toppled forward, just as Steele shot directly into its open mouth. The bullet went in at an upward angle, striking more teeth and then hitting the small brain, chewing it up some more before exiting out the rear of the skull, taking a trail of brains with it.

As the beast fell, Steele jumped to the side, the massive carcass barely missing crushing his leg. He rolled onto his side and came up in a crouch, prepared to fire the last of his bullets if he had to. But it was painfully clear the battle was over, and in this particular fight, man had overcome beast.

Steele wasn't taking any chances, however. He pulled his hunting knife from his hip and jumped onto the lizard's back, then began stabbing it again and again. Dark ichor flew off in all directions as he continued to stab it. Tears flowed down his cheeks as he vented his rage at losing Kim, and for a full two minutes all he did was slice the carcass to shreds. Raising his arm high, he plunged the knife in again and again until his arm was practically numb from each blow.

He didn't hear the professor calling his name for almost thirty seconds, and only when the older man went and stood directly in front of Steele was he finally pulled from his haze of hate and loss and back to reality.

The professor was screaming something but his voice was quickly drowned out. There was rumbling, a rushing sound that overrode everything else. Then Steele saw what the professor was yelling at him about as the older man pointed off in the distance, from where he and Steele had come from before climbing the hill.

The tidal wave had arrived.

The wave struck the hill so hard the entire plateau shuddered, as if it was nothing more than an anthill caught in a sudden rainstorm. Refuse in the wave struck the hill as well, taking massive chunks of dirt out of the sides. The water rose quickly, and before Steele or the professor could do anything, Kim's still body was caught up in the rising flood waters and pulled off the plateau. Both men tried to grab her as she was taken away, but she was gone so fast there was no time. Next went the mutant lizard. Its carcass was lifted and it floated away to disappear under the water when it reached the edge of the plateau.

The two men stood fast together, each supporting the other. Neither knew how high the water would get. If it rose much higher then both would join their fallen friend, drowning in the churning water.

But the rising level stopped when it was at the men's knees of the initial wave, and as each second passed, it leveled off, then began to recede so that only a foot of the hill was above the water. Bracing themselves against the current and doing their best to avoid any detritus that could knock them over, they fought the current and remained firm until the water wasn't on the plateau anymore.

Many of the animals on the hill weren't so lucky and were washed away into the floodtide to be lost from sight at the first onslaught.

Those that were tall and heavy enough to withstand the water's pull, huddled together, snorting and mewling in fear, eyes looking anxiously at the water as it rose to their chests and above. Once more, hunter and prey huddled together, each making a brief truce with one another over the common enemy.

As the wave passed and the water level dropped so that all remaining on the hill were safe, more screaming animals that were in the fast flowing current floated past the hill, along with even more debris. The sound was horrible, all the barking, growling and roars as hundreds of animals were sucked into the cold depths. Some tried to climb onto the floating wreckage, but many were too heavy and were soon lost among the waves once more.

Steele watched it all in silence, knowing if he and the professor hadn't found the hill, they would surely be dead by now.

A huge, waterlogged tree drifted by, a family of raccoons and beavers attached to it. Each had eyes wide in fear as they held onto the uprooted tree.

For more than three hours the water roared past, and then finally began to recede for good, the level steadily dropping until there was barely ten feet on the ground, then five, and then only one. The water was slowly absorbed into the already waterlogged ground. Soon, only muddy pools of dirty water could be seen where the ground had dips and valleys.

Animal carcasses were everywhere and every kind of refuse imaginable. There was the roof of a house fifty feet away as well as a damaged boat, and more cars and pickup trucks than Steele had seen in a long time in one place. It was too bad every one of them was destroyed and waterlogged; most had no tires or glass for windows, and many had no engines.

The animals on the plateau, sensing it was time to leave, each headed off, scampering down the ragged side of the hill in different directions, more than a few losing their footing and tumbling down the hard way. A few didn't get up after landing, no doubt having snapped their necks in the fall like ones before them.

Steele did the same, seeing it was time to leave, and he gathered whatever he could that hadn't been taken by the flood. He found Kim's .45, where it had become stuck in the wet sand, and he picked it up and slid it into his waistband. It was all he had left of the woman he loved.

"Sorry about your bag of books, Prof," he said when he realized the pack had been taken away by the floodwaters.

"That's quite all right, dear boy. You did your best. I shall find more and start a new collection, rest assure to that."

Steele only grunted in response as he moved to the edge of the plateau, ready to make the climb down. "Keep your butt on the face of the hill as you slide down, Prof. If you don't, you'll end up going ass over elbow and there's no telling how you'll land."

"Hard I suppose," the professor said softly.

"I'll go down first and then if you do mess it up, maybe I can catch you before you break your neck." Before the older man could respond, Steele was over the edge and sliding down the hill.

The side wasn't as steep as it was before, thanks to the erosion of the floodwaters and Steele made it to the ground easily. The professor did as he was instructed and made it more than halfway before one of his feet hit a rock and he found himself knocked off balance. But Steele was as good as his word, and when the older man began to roll down the hill uncontrollably, Steele was there to help his landing. Both men ended up in a heap, and Steele rose without saying a word. The professor muttered a brief thank you and left it at that. He knew his friend was hurting from the loss of Kim and he didn't want to push Steele till the man was ready. He knew the grizzled warrior wouldn't show his true feelings and perhaps when he was ready he might discuss it. But no doubt the wound was far too fresh to make him speak of it yet.

His cane had made the fall intact and the professor leaned on it, glad to have it with him.

Steele was checking his sawed-off, knowing it would need a full stripping, cleaning and oiling when they found a safe place to camp for the night, as would all their weapons.

"You ready?" Steele asked the professor as he prepared to head out.

"Yes, Martin, as ready as I can be given our present circumstances."

"Good, let's go. We need to get clear of the area. With all these dead animals exposed to the sun, it's gonna get real ripe real fast around here."

The professor only nodded as the two men began to walk.

"We'll make a quick camp and try and get a fire going as soon as we find someplace dry," Steele said. "We need to dry our footwear or else we risk getting trench foot or worse."

"An excellent idea, Martin. I agree wholeheartedly," the professor said.

The two men walked in silence, only the squishing of their boots on the wet ground breaking the quiet. An hour passed with neither man speaking. The sun was high and the ground was drying fast.

By tomorrow, it would be like the flood had never happened, with the exception of all the wreckage.

Destruction was everywhere, and more than one human body was seen as the two men crossed the expanse. Steele's eyes focused on each corpse, hoping, yet not hoping, that one of them would be Kim's.

He would have liked to have given her a proper burial. The thought of her body hanging from some gnarled tree miles away to rot in the sun, birds pecking out her eyes and tongue, made him so angry he thought he would explode.

The world he lived in was a hard one, a place where death could take a person at any time in ways too many to list, and though he and Kim had accepted this as their reality, to lose her so suddenly was still difficult to reconcile. He kept thinking if he turned around she would be there, walking along quietly. When she would see he was looking at her she would smile and wink, perhaps brushing her hair from her face as a casual gesture.

Steele was pulled from his thoughts to find the professor was asking him something. "Huh, what did you say?"

"I said, do you have a destination in mind for us, Martin?"

"No, not really. For now I just want to get out of this blasted flood area and onto dry ground. Is that okay with you?" Normally his tone wouldn't have come across as harsh as it did, but the anger he felt at Kim's loss was an overriding factor. He was so damn frustrated without a way to vent it all, so it was pent up inside him, a massive thunderstorm of anger, grief, hate and loss, all rolled into one massive storm.

Like the professor knew this, the older man let the tone slide as if he hadn't heard it. "Yes, dear boy, of course it is." He used his cane to push aside something particularly nasty, not wanting to step in it. "And may I make a suggestion?" When Steele didn't reply, he continued. "When we find a place to camp for the night, would you mind if I say a few words to mourn Kim? I miss her terribly."

Steele's eyes softened and he nodded curtly. "That would be nice, Prof. I know she would've liked that."

The professor reached out and squeezed Steele's arm as a father would to a son, then he withdrew it and patted Steele on the shoulder.

"She was a good woman, Martin, and she gave her life saving you. If she could do it again, I have no doubt she would, despite the consequences. She was a brave woman."

Steele nodded once more, the hint of a tear in the corner of his right eye. "Yeah Prof, you're probably right on that one. Come on, let's keep moving, we have a lot of ground to cover before it gets dark."

The older man smiled wanly and the two warriors set off once more, now minus one of their own. What the future held for them over the horizon was anyone's guess.

But whatever awaited them, the two friends would deal with it head on, with a loaded gun in one hand and a sharpened blade in the other.

STAGE DONE

MICHAEL D. GRIFFITHS

David Dellis checked his gun one more time. He only had three bullets left. He was alone, all of his friends now dead.

A sound echoed up from the canyon. He cursed himself for speaking aloud and then kept moving. The Pariah River should only be a few more miles away and he needed water almost as badly as escaping from the freaks that followed him.

Ellie had called them freaks, until she'd become one of them. She was the last of his friends to go. They had been lovers at the end, before she'd mutated like everyone else. Thoughts of her almost brought tears to his eyes. He missed her the most, but after two months of total isolation, he would have been happy to see his worst enemy as long as they weren't infected.

The problem was…everyone had the plague.

He probably had it too; it was just a strange quirk that found him immune. Sometimes, he felt it was far more of a curse than a blessing.

David heard the sounds again—a stray pebble being ground into the sandstone, a grunt drifting up through the wind.

He kept moving.

David always tried to keep to the high ground, anything to give him an advantage. When the entire world was after you, any advantage you could get was necessary. Breaths came to him in gasps as he pushed himself harder. As the elevation rose, the air grew thinner, but nothing felt as bad as the heat, except maybe the lack of water.

He knew he wasn't going to be able to fight them off unless he got something to drink first. Looking back, he saw what had to be nearly a dozen nappy heads bobbing up and down as they jogged after him.

After a few tortuous minutes of travel, the canyon grew more narrow and steep. He slowed as he used both hands to aid his assent. Soon, he was climbing more than running. Behind him, the mutants grew closer.

He'd almost reached the top of the jagged cliff, when the freaks let out a series of howling. They had spotted their prey. David was never sure why they were always so hell-bent on killing everything in their path. Was it jealousy? Did they hate what they had become? Did survivors like David remind them of what they once were? He, of course, had no idea. He just knew the facts. The freaks killed any living organism they came across with the exception of each other.

The mutants headed over the rough boulders after him. The freaks had the advantage of a complete disregard for their own well-being. David had seen them snap fingers in attempts to open car doors or less-healthy freaks sprint after him until they gave themselves heart attacks. They never stopped. It was the main reason he'd chosen to try to live in such a remote area. At least here, their numbers were few or should have been.

"I shouldn't have tried to go to Lee's Ferry for supplies," he mumbled between gasps. *How could I have been so stupid? I guess I'll pay for wanting to eat something besides desert rat*, he thought.

Somehow, he reached the upper edge of the canyon. Once he climbed over the rise, he looked around in wonder. The plateau stretched out before him, flat and without so much as a tree to hide behind.

Looking back, he saw the freaks were only a hundred feet behind him. *Shit. Looks like I won't be finding a better place to make a stand,* he thought. He gritted his teeth as he readied himself. Picking up a head-sized rock; he raised it above him. "Chew on this, you fuckers!" He threw it at the crowd with all his strength.

The first rock missed hitting anything, but the second resulted in a head shot, the skull cracking so loudly that the noise echoed through the canyon.

The mob grew closer, so he just threw rock after rock as quickly as he could. He wasn't picky what he hit. Rocks that would come loose went down at them, as well. Small avalanches started and many of the freaks took serious wounds when they toppled several yards over the harsh terrain; even if they broke an arm, they would leap back up and race up the hill again.

Steam rose from their spilled blood and its foul toxic odor filled the air. That was one of the reasons David couldn't afford to let them reach him; all the infected had mutated blood. Their blood, as well as spittle, had become dangerous weapons. Where once normal bodily fluid flowed through them, now their veins were filled with some strange type of dangerous acid.

David wasn't sure how this acidic blood didn't dissolve through their flesh, but that never seemed to happen. The liquid wasn't as strong as hydrochloric acid, it wouldn't dissolve through metal and the like, but it would certainly burn through human flesh. David had the burn scars to prove it. He'd seen men blinded by the mutant's spittle and other such tragedies. The important thing was to kill them before they could reach you, and if you had to use hand-to-hand combat, blunt weapons were better than blades. That was why David always carried a baseball bat for back up. Something he certainly hoped he wouldn't have to use today.

David had to search further and further for rocks to throw as he used up his surrounding supply. At least the freaks became easier to hit as they got closer, but they were almost upon him. He threw a few last rocks, drew his pistol and unstrapped his bat. He wondered if he should use his last bullets now or save them.

Gazing down, he saw that there were six remaining freaks. Normally, this would be more than enough to overwhelm him, but he had the high ground. "Screw it," he said under his breath and stuffed his pistol back into his belt.

He brought down his bat onto the center of the first freak's head. It went tumbling back, dead long before it hit the bottom of the ravine. His next victim not only fell, but took a young female back down the canyon with it.

He wound up for his next swing, but before it could land home on a black-haired freak, a hand caught him by the ankle. The only way he could avoid being spread over the boulders below was to drop back on his butt.

The hand kept pulling him toward the edge until his bat cracked the mutant's knuckles hard enough to break fingers. The grip was released, but the other two freaks had climbed over the rise.

He tossed his bat at the closer one's face. It barely did more than make it grunt. The second rushed toward him, spitting as it came.

The caustic drool splattered David's shoulder and the side of his right cheek, causing him to cry out as his flesh sizzled. As he fumbled for his pistol, the third freak was crawling over the edge. That one received a boot to the face, which luckily sent it tumbling back down into the canyon with a startled scream.

Two quick shots hit the spitter in the chest and it crashed to the ground with an animalistic moan.

The last one leapt upon David. Its fingers clawed at him like a wild cat. Only his jean jacket saved him from serious injury. Its hands moved for David's throat, but he pulled his gun and placed the muzzle of the pistol against its skull, then sent one of his last remaining bullets into its head at point-blank range.

He screamed as the acidic blood from blowback splattered his hair and forehead.

The pain was intense. He tried to catch his breath but it wouldn't come. Black dots filled his vision and he slipped into darkness.

When David awoke the stars were out. No moon graced the sky and the stars seemed impossibly bright. He rose slowly and dusted himself off.

His skin was tight and inflamed where the acid had burned him. Half his head and face throbbed with pain, but he would survive.

He found his pistol in the dirt. He put it into his backpack. The baseball bat was on the incline and he went down to get it, his dehydration becoming his chief concern as he moved.

His mouth felt like he'd been chewing on sandpaper. Looking around, he saw no sign of movement.

"At least I killed all of you bastards," he yelled, while kicking one of the bodies back into the ravine. A moaning traveled up to him and he froze in terror. Were there more of them? Then he realized it had come from two mutants too battered and injured to move. "Serves you assholes right. Messing with me," he chuckled, his voice hoarse.

He climbed down off the incline and headed down into the canyon, then began moving to the river. It felt like the longest two miles of his life, but eventually he made it to the slow waters of the Pariah.

There was nothing dangerous around, or tracks that told him anything had been in the area for some time. Enough vegetation grew along the banks that he had no problem building a fire. Reaching into his backpack, he took out and opened a can of peas.

He ate the can slowly, relishing every bite. With a full stomach, sleep claimed him easily and for the first time in weeks, he closed his eyes feeling safe.

Three weeks had passed since his botched raid on Lee's Ferry and his battle at the cliff. His face had healed to the point that it no longer troubled him, but his hair was still patchy and he doubted he'd be winning any beauty contests.

What the hell does it matter how I look? he thought. *It's not like I'll be finding any women to ask to the movies these days. Hell, I probably won't be seeing a living soul that isn't a mutated freak for the rest of my life.*

His stomach growled loud enough to start a rock slide and he scooped up a can full of water in the hopes to fill it with something. It didn't really help.

The canned food had run out over a week ago. He'd tried to live off frogs and fish, but catching them was almost impossible with his limited equipment. The few fish he caught were small and were just enough to keep him going.

He knew he couldn't go on like this forever. Then he thought of something. The mutants couldn't grow or harvest food. All they did was hunt. Since they didn't eat each other, they must be wasting away by now.

It had been over three months since the plague started. No human being could last that long without food. And if they did survive, they would have to be living off of animals, which would mean they would be out at the farms and in the woods, not the cities. It would be a risk that the cities were deserted, but one worth taking.

Shouldering his pack and casting one last look at the campsite, he headed out for Cedar City.

Once David drew within sight of Cedar City, he stopped in his tracks. The mid-sized town was surrounded by a formidable wall. Everything from tree trunks to eighteen wheelers had been used to create it. Outside of the walls, hundreds of bodies and vehicles had been left to slowly decay in the desert sun.

Even more shocking was that after a few minutes of staring, he spotted a man with a rifle walk by on the inner part of the wall, like he was on patrol. David remained indecisive for nearly an hour, but then decided to make himself known. He was at the point that he would rather die than live the rest of his life alone and the prospect of more people was too much to ignore.

With his decision made, he walked toward the wall with his hands raised above his head. "Hail the wall!" he shouted. He repeated the phrase twice more as he approached. He made it to within fifty feet of the wall when a shot rang out and a bullet created a small puff of dust a foot before his feet.

"Stay right there! What do you want?" an angry voice called down to him.

"Just hearing you speak those words aloud is more than I've dared to hope for all these weeks."

"How do I know you aren't one of those things?"

"I'm talking…"

"Don't get smart with me, boy. You stay right there. Don't come any closer. I'm gonna have to check with some folks."

After what seemed like an eternity, a different voice called down to him. "Hello there, stranger. What do you call yourself?" The voice sounded older and had an air of quiet confidence about it.

"I'm David."

"What sort of man are you?"

David found that question odd and for a moment was uncertain what to say, but settled for, "A pretty normal one, I guess. I used to be a carpenter, if that matters."

"Well, we can never get enough of those. How do I know you aren't infected?"

David could see the man a little. He might have been about sixty, with a close cropped head of gray hair.

"I think I'm immune for whatever reason. I was living in Phoenix before. If I didn't get mutated there, I doubt it can happen. I've been clawed, bit, and spit upon, and nothing's happened. From my experience, people who get infected start mutating within a few hours."

"That's my understanding, too. Come closer."

David did as he was asked.

"So you're immune to the plague? That could come in handy, even more so than you being a carpenter. You may approach the wall, David. We'll lower a rope for you."

After being led through a strangely standard looking town, David was brought into a large temple. Along the way, all faces had turned to watch him. His scarred visage had brought a hush over the quickly gathering crowd and the looks he received ranged from awe and fear to outright hostility.

The town itself was a weird mix of jury-rigged vehicles and other modern devices, all working together with more primitive technology. This gave the town a weird feeling, like a place out of the Wild West or some futuristic Steam Punk world. The men and women looked similar, and all were Caucasian.

Most of the men were armed and kept a close watch on David, like we was about to somehow go crazy with just his fists. The women gave him a wide birth. The older man that had spoken to him before was called Thomas and he was both the Pastor and also the leader of the townspeople.

Once they'd settled in the church, David was brought to a back room, and served a delightful chicken dinner. He had a hard time not devouring it like a starved wolf. Only Thomas joined him at the table, if not in the meal. Another six well-armed men leaned against the wall, as if they were guarding him. David couldn't help but wonder what they thought he could do that would require him to be so heavily watched.

Thomas made harmless chit-chat until David had finished eating. He asked about where David had been, and how he'd made it this far north.

"Not much to tell, really," David answered. "I drove most of the way, trying to avoid any place that had cities or towns. The bridge at Marble Canyon is destroyed and I had a hell of a time making it down those cliffs and across the Colorado, but once I was on this side, I figured I was within one of the most desolated areas in America. That sounded good to me."

"So you say you're immune to the infection?"

"Yeah, ah…I guess so. I'd have to be, right? The disease spreads so quickly. I would've been a freak months ago, otherwise."

"How do we know he isn't working for them?" a dark-haired man with a shotgun demanded.

"Work for who, the freaks?" David asked. "Those things don't even *talk*, and they kill everything on sight. How could I be working for them? Besides, you guys seem safe here. Hell, I bet I probably hate them ten times more than you. I had to fight my way through hundreds of miles to get here." Looking around, he waved with a hand to signify the town. "I'm surprised this place even exists. Actually talking to another human, let alone how many of you are here, well, it seems like a dream."

"Let's put such issues aside for a moment," Thomas said, keeping his voice calm. "In a perfect world, what would you like to see happen now?"

David shifted in his seat. "Uh, would it be okay if I stayed here? It's been so long since I've been with others. I honestly thought I'd never talk to another human again."

"Sir," the man with the shotgun said to Thomas. "Do we really want to take in any riff-raff that shows up at our gate to stay here? Having them looking at our wives and chasing our daughters and who knows what else?"

"Well, Miller, from the sounds of things, there aren't too many lonely souls left out there," Thomas said. "I think we owe humanity a certain obligation, don't you?" Turning back to David, he said, "And if this gentleman is immune to the plague, perhaps we could devise some type of serum from his blood. He could protect our wives and daughters. Who knows, maybe we could even catch the mutants and restore them, as well."

Miller just grunted, while his eyes continued to bore into David's.

"May I ask a question?"

"Certainly, David."

"I've been wondering about how long the freaks can stay alive. These are still living people, after all. They need to eat and drink, and since they don't eat each other, might it be possible that they'll die off sooner or later? I mean, I'd think they'd be crawling over your walls to get in here, but I didn't have to fight a single one."

"We had them showing up for quite a while, but we would always shoot them right away," Thomas said. "Our wall isn't impenetrable, of course. But yes, they seem to be becoming fewer and fewer. However, we have noted that they will feed on their fallen fellows, so in the big cities, they could be lingering on for quite some time as they continue to engage in their cannibalistic ways."

"I see. I was also wondering if…" David began but was cut off.

"Perhaps we should save further questions until you're well rested and ah, shaved and showered, my friend. Not to be cruel, but you stink rather badly. We have a few hotels in Cedar City and I'm sure we can find you an empty room." Thomas smiled. "You'll be happy to discover we still have hot running water."

"That sounds like heaven, thank you."

"Then follow me, please," Thomas said.

David was led out of the church and to a hotel a block over. The woman behind the desk smiled at him politely and got David settled, Thomas leaving him to rest.

"I'll have someone wake you for dinner. There is still so much to discuss," Thomas said as he and his men departed. David looked out onto the street from his room and he saw three men standing out there, as if they were guarding the building. He had no doubt there were some in back as well. He opened his door that led into hallway and he saw a man on each end also. Deciding for the moment he was too tired to care, he closed the door and began to strip, eager to shower.

A full fifteen minutes later, he emerged from the steaming shower feeling better than he had in months. There were a hundred questions he wanted to ask, but when he lay on the soft bed—his stomach full, as well as being clean—he felt drowsy.

Sleep claimed him almost immediately, even before he could even pull the blanket over him.

Something jarred him awake. He couldn't be sure what it was until it sounded again. A scream. It was quickly followed by another and then another. Soon, a chorus of cries filled the night. He rushed to the window while hurrying into his jeans, which were still filthy. They felt terrible on his clean skin but he ignored it.

It would be just my luck that the place would be attacked the night I showed up, he thought, but then quickly discovered this wasn't the case. The citizens of Cedar City had gone crazy and were slaughtering each other. "Oh no," he gasped. "They've gotten the plague."

Behind him, the door to his hotel was kicked open. Miller was there, still armed with his shotgun. Blood mixed with sweat across his forehead. David knew the man was already infected, but had not quite crossed over yet into full-blown madness.

"You stupid piece of shit! You doomed us all. You brought the plague into our sanctuary!" Miller screamed, spittle flying from his mouth.

David backed away with his arms in the air. "I didn't know. I'm sorry."

"You might be immune, but you're a carrier! You killed us all!"

"I didn't mean to. I didn't know, I swear!"

"That doesn't matter now. But I'll be damned if I'm gonna let you live after killing my town!"

He was raising his shotgun to take aim when two female freaks rushed in and grabbed him from behind. "No!" he shouted. "I'm your father, let me go!"

David didn't hesitate. While Miller fought, he ran forward and snatched the shotgun from him. Three blasts later, the father and his daughters' blood mixed in an ever expanding pool on the floor.

After grabbing his pack, David rushed out of the room. The streets were in chaos. He kept to the shadows and headed to the nearest wall. He had to use the shotgun twice, but there were still enough normal people left that the mutants had other targets to attack. Despite this, a small gang of freaks soon spotted him and gave chase. He reached the wall at the cost of emptying the shotgun. He tossed it aside and climbed a ladder with at least ten of the newly-born mutants right on his heels.

He pushed the ladder away from the fence as soon as he reached the top of the wall, and the three freaks climbing up it cried out in alarm as they crashed back into the pavement below. Others were already climbing the wall from other ladders, so he hurried to the other side. After dropping to the ground, he sprinted away from the town as fast as he could.

The mutants followed, not wanting to let their prey escape. David had a hundred foot lead on them, but this time his pursuers were well fed and he knew he couldn't outlast them.

Then he spotted a bicycle lying on the side of the road. As he got closer, he saw blood splattered around it. The owner was long gone, probably killed, but the bike was still intact.

For once a bit of luck was thrown his way as he picked up the bike and hopped on it, then began to pedal as fast as his legs would allow. He flicked the gears so the pedaling became easier, and he shot down the road like a bullet, weaving in and around any stalled vehicles or debris.

The freaks ran after him, but they couldn't keep up with a man on a bicycle, and soon they fell behind and were lost from sight. An hour later, he drew in a deep breath and almost laughed when he saw a sign for a place called Zion.

Seems like as good a place as any, he thought.

The bicycle had a small mirror attached to the handle bar and a little headlight, which was connected to the tire and when it was on, the tire generated the power for it. David stared at his scarred face in the small mirror for a moment as moonlight bathed the area in its pallid glow, then he flicked on the small headlight.

It was the only sign of illumination in his dark world.

THE BOTANIST'S CURSE

P. A. DOUGLAS

Monday *9:31 a.m. – Central Time*

"I'm telling you, Professor, this is going to work!" Ming was excited. "I've tested the results myself!"

Prof. Barton took his eyes away from the computer. Glaring at his Asian assistant over the frame of his spectacles, he laughed. "I've heard you sing a similar tune before, my friend." Barton took his glasses off, laying them on the keyboard before him. "What makes you think this trial run is going to be any different than the last batch of tests?"

Prof. Barton had been the leading botanist in the country for almost a decade, and with his new Asian assistant, Ming, Barton was breaking even more ground with new discoveries daily.

Ming was a brilliant asset for sure, but was clumsy at times, but Prof. Barton was happy to take the young man under his wing. Show him a thing or two. Ming just needed to slow down and realize results didn't happen overnight.

But then again…wasn't that what this series of lab tests were all about? Altering the result time on plant growth?

"All right, Ming, let's see the results from last night's preliminary screenings." Prof. Barton stood up and put his glasses back on. "It's a little soon to be excited, don't you think? We shouldn't see any real improvement for another day or so."

As they made their way through the office area and down the hall to the main lab, Ming couldn't wipe his silly grin off his face.

His cheeks were plump with anticipation. Once they'd made their way into the green house, Barton's mouth dropped open.

Taken aback, he said, "Wow, are these really the results from last night's run? It's incredible!"

"Yes, sir." Ming bounced in place. Struggling to keep still, the enthusiasm had him.

Reaching down, the professor plucked a ripe strawberry. He sniffed it. Bouncing it in his hands like a baseball, his eyes grew wide. "My word, this has got to be at least a third in size from yesterday." He looked at Ming. "Are you messing with me?"

"No, sir. That's the same one from last night. Scouts honor."

"Come on, don't even give me that. You weren't even in the scouts."

They both laughed, even joked with exhilaration. They had done it. The growth serum worked, and faster than Prof. Barton ever could have expected. This could mean the end to world hunger.

"Nobel Prize, here we come!" Prof. Barton laughed and bit into the strawberry with enthusiasm, red juice gushing from his lips to roll down his chin. The flavor was unreal, so fresh and sweet.

*M*onday 8:07 p.m. – *Central Time*

That night, the professor and his staff of ten men and women celebrated. Wine and cocktails were served up with cigars and laughter. All of their hard work had finally paid off. The downtown bar they all met at was thriving with life as the night edged on, but that wasn't the only thing beginning to thrive to life.

Little did they know, things weren't as under control as they hoped back at the lab. In the green house, plants were stirring, growing and mutating. Next to the strawberry plant were several other plants also treated with the same chemicals. Deep inside a set of tomatoes, one little worm began to fester. This small, insignificant worm had been treated with the same chemicals as the strawberry.

It started growing rapidly.

With no one left to attend the lab or the growing worm, things began to go wrong—very wrong. Over the course of only a few hours, the worm grew five times its natural size. No longer confined to the inside of the tomato, it now roamed the green house, feasting on all of the plants in sight. As a result, it grew larger and became hungrier, and each plant consumed that was infused with the growth serum only made it become larger.

It quickly became something more than a worm. It became aggressive.

It wasn't long before it was out of food, having eaten everything in the greenhouse. The mammoth worm thrashed about, agitated and hungry, as pots of soil and tables with flowers on them were obliterated under the weight of the growing creature. Soon, the greenhouse structure began to buckle. The worm pressed against the walls, wanting to be free. Glass shattered. Bursting free from the greenhouse, the worm made its way outside. It squirmed its way across the dark, empty parking lot unnoticed. A trail of slime trailed behind.

It wasn't long before it found the lawn and the soft soil beneath.

The massive worm plowed into the ground, filling the hole behind it and leaving a pile of soil that would have the gardener scratching his head in confusion the following morning. Digging deep into the soft earth, the worm came to rest in a warm place only ten feet below the surface. Motionless and tired, it rested, though it kept growing in size.

Before the night was over, the giant worm had grown to nearly eighteen feet long and six feet wide. Filled with too much of the growth serum, the creature's body couldn't handle the rapid growth and began to feed on itself. Hours later, it trembled once and expired.

But it wasn't over. While rotting underground, other insects and worms began to feed on the massive carcass. The mutated worm had become lunch for an endless sea of its kind.

Tuesday 7:46 a.m. – Central Time

"What in God's name happened here?" Prof. Barton was livid as he stared at what was left of the greenhouse.

"You tell me, sir," the police officer said, looking down at the note pad in his hand; he readied his pen. "Do you have any enemies, Mr. Barton?"

"That's Professor Barton and no, of course not. You must be joking."

"Do I look like I'm joking?" The officer stared at him with pen in hand.

The greenhouse had been utterly destroyed. There was no vegetation left. Not knowing what had happened, he assumed all his plants had been stolen and the place wrecked to cover any evidence by the thieves. Though how the thieves managed to bring down the roof was beyond him. He also couldn't explain the large slime trail leading away from the greenhouse.

"Can you explain to us what this stuff is, Prof. Barton?" The officer pointed down at the trail of slime. "It leads off to the parking lot."

"Then what?" Ming asked, walking up to join the conversation.

"Then nothing," the cop said. "The trail just ends in the grass, past the lot."

"What do you mean it just ends?"

"Like I said, 'it just ends.' We have some of our men looking into it. There's a large pile of dirt there and a place where it looks like the soil has been turned over, but I don't know what that might mean."

Prof. Barton looked away from the officer and gazed over at the slime trail.

"Prof. Barton, I'm going to ask again. Do you have any enemies that would want to come in and vandalize this place?"

The professor ignored the question. "Show me this pile of dirt, please. Maybe it'll give me an idea as to who could have done this."

The officer shrugged. "Fine, follow me."

As they followed the slime trail, the officer continued to ask the professor questions about his work. When the dirt pile came in sight, Prof. Barton saw that there were a few more policemen inspecting the dirt and overturned soil. It was obvious none of the cops took the area to be anything important and were just going through the numbers until they could leave.

Suddenly, the earth began to shake!

"Earthquake!" someone shouted, spilling their coffee as everyone swayed and pivoted off balance.

"We've had earthquakes before, but this one's bad!" Ming shouted, having fallen to the ground. "When is it going to stop?"

Before Prof. Barton could respond, the first worm burst forth from the ground. A brown, slimy earthworm the size of a refrigerator tore through the soil.

Exploding the dirt around it, the mutated beastworm rose ten feet in height before crashing down to the ground. The massive load of its girth landed atop a squad car, flattening it, the passenger inside instantly crushed to death. Blood dripped out of the demolished metal frame to pool on the pavement.

"What the hell is…" Prof. Barton was cut off when another giant worm burst forth from the ground, then another and another. The professor and Ming watched in horror as hundreds of worms surfaced. Already mutated beyond their normal size, they were still growing…as was their hunger. Snapping forward, the worms began to attack the terrified humans, snapping them up and swallowing them whole. One cop was dragged away screaming, his body hidden to the waist by the orifice of a worm.

The report of a shotgun rang out.

"Look. Over there!" Ming pointed.

Two policemen were tucked behind their squad car, firing at the worms. A giant worm was headed right for them, seeming to ignore the barrage of buckshot it was receiving. The men kept firing, but compared to the worm's size, the damage was insignificant. The shots were like little pin pricks as they entered the undulating skin. In seconds, the worm was on them, swallowing each screaming man whole.

Prof. Barton turned to see the cop that had been questioning him running away. In full sprint, the man in blue disappeared around the corner of the wrecked greenhouse.

"Could this be something we did, Professor?" Ming was still on the ground in shock. "Do you think it had something to do with our growth serum?"

Prof. Barton scanned the scene around them, but before he could process what Ming had suggested, the ground right under the two men began to shake. A worm surged forth from the ground, swallowing both men instantly. They didn't even see it coming and all that was left were the professors' eyeglasses which had fallen from his face as he had been sucked up.

Soon, thousands of giant worms began to surface all over the city, devouring everything in sight. Others didn't surface right away, but burrowed underground. Traveling for countless miles in search for food, their quest would never end.

Where they surfaced would be anyone's guess.

*T*wo Months Later – Time Unknown

"What are we going to do, Tom?" Kate asked, her voice filled with dread. "We're almost out of food!"

"Shhh…" Tim put his finger to his lips and whispered, "Keep your voice down. You think I don't know that? We've survived this long, haven't we? You need to have faith. We're gonna make it. Trust me, all right. We just need to stay calm and stick together."

"But how are we going to live if we can't go out and scavenge for food?" Kate tossed an empty can of refried beans across the small room. The metal can clinked against the wall before coming to rest on the floor.

"Stop that! Are you crazy? You want those things to know we're in here? Is that it?" Tom grabbed Kate by the wrist. "Look…sooner or later those things are gonna realize there isn't any more food for them in this region. Once they do, they'll be on their way. You know they're sensitive to vibrations! So tossing crap around and raising your voice is doing nothing but prolonging the inevitable. As long as they sense we're here, they aren't gonna leave." He calmed down slightly and kissed her on the forehead. "I love you, Kate. We just need to wait this thing out, okay?"

She nodded. "I know. I'm sorry."

"We are running low on food and supplies. But if we ration them a little more, we can make them last a few more weeks. Maybe by then the worms will be gone."

Kate pulled away, angry. "Ration them some more? I'm already starving as it is! Look at me, Tom. I've lost more than thirty pounds for Christ's sake."

Glaring at Tom, she crossed her boney arms.

"Fine. Do whatever the hell you want. I'm out of here." He turned away from her and stormed out of the room.

"Wait, where are you going?" she whimpered.

"The roof. I need some time to think. I'll be back later."

He slammed the door on his way out and instantly regretted it. Surely the worms felt that one underground. It was loud, but it was too late to take it back now. Kate just didn't understand. She was lucky to even be alive. They both were. When the worm wars first started, he and Kate had been on their way to New Mexico.

Passing through Texas was a long haul. That was when they had first heard of the attacks on the radio. Stopping in to get gas at a hole-in-the-wall, middle-of-nowhere gas station, they had seen it firsthand on television. People in the streets were overrun by the giant worms. It had been Tom's idea to make for the roof of the station. It was what had saved their lives. They had sat there and watched people die on that roof. But what else could they have done? It had been devastating for them both.

Nearly a month later and they were still at the gas station. They'd tried to make a run for it five times, but each time had almost cost them their lives. The worms reacted to vibrations, and before they had time to reach their car parked outside, it would be too late, and the worms would surface. The only thing they could do was wait.

Kate was terrified, and so was Tom, but he also counted his blessings. At least they had found themselves trapped in a place with food and beverages. The place was filled with the items found in a convenience store. And being in the middle of nowhere was a good thing, too. They had learned over the radio in the last few weeks that the more populated areas had become overrun, but with no one around to make noise and stir things up, the amount of worms was much lower around the gas station. Nothing but desert and highway surrounded it. Tom was thankful for that.

Reaching the gas station's roof, Tom stared up into the night sky. Amazed by how bright the stars were, he found himself lost in them. With no lights to drown out their beauty, they lit up the night like flickering specks of candlelight.

He sighed. Kate was right. They needed to do something, and soon. All of the perishables in the gas station were gone, as they had eaten those first before the power went out. It had been a small gas station and the supplies were limited, and even two people can eat a lot when there is nothing else to do to keep occupied. Kate had read every magazine in the place more than once and Tom had perused the same periodical repeatedly.

He sat down on the chair he had placed on the roof and began to look at the sea of sand and highway. In the distance, he spotted the ripple of disturbed earth. Focusing his eyes into the darkness, he could see them against the moonlight. They were searching for food. When the sun went down they were more inclined to come out of the ground. How much longer *would* it be before they moved on? He wondered how was the rest of the world was holding up. From what he'd heard on the radio from the surrounding areas… it wasn't good.

He reached over and clicked on the AM/FM battery-powered radio.

With the volume low, his ears filled with the sound of white noise. Nothing but static.

He flipped through the channels. It had been more than a week since the last broadcast and what he'd heard hadn't been good. The people manning the radio station had run out of food and water and were talking about going out to scout for more supplies.

There was a grocery store near them. The announcer said that they would work their way back to the radio station once they had what they needed. Tom was glad and hoped they had made it. All this time it had helped him keep his sanity just to hear other people's voices, to know he and Kate weren't the last ones left alive, as unbelievable as that sounded.

But he had to wonder long could it seriously take to stock up and get back to the radio station.

Defeated, he turned off the radio, wanting to save the batteries.

Chances were they hadn't even made it to the grocery store. The worms had probably gotten them for sure. Tom began to become stressed, thinking about his chances for survival. They were slim and he knew it. But he needed to stay strong; if not for himself than for Kate. Lighting up a cigarette, he smiled as the smoke left his lips.

At least he wouldn't be running out of cigarettes any time soon. The funny thing was that he and Kate hadn't been smokers before all of this. Hardly ever drank for that matter, too. But that had all changed. Everything had. With the worms out there, the dangers of smoking and drinking seemed kind of silly.

He silently puffed away at his menthol, trying to come up with a plan, a way to get by just a little longer. He ran his fingers through his greasy hair.

His body odor was strong from lack of bathing and he knew it, but what was there to do? He sure as hell wasn't about to try running the water. The pipes, they ran underground.

When he finished the cigarette, he closed his eyes and fell asleep on the roof.

Tom suddenly woke to the sound of rushing water and the rising sun. He jumped up from his chair, panicked, then darted across the roof and quietly made his way down the ladder and back into the gas station. The sound of gushing water from inside the building grew louder.

"What's going on, Kate?"

Kate jumped into his arms the moment he entered.

"I don't know!" she shouted. "Something happened!"

"What do you mean, 'you don't know'? What happened?" He shook her, trying to get a straight answer.

All she could mutter was, "The toilet…the toilet." Her voice was shaky.

"Oh no…" Tom ran to the bathroom at the back of the station, kicking the door open.

The toilet and sink were both gushing out a torrential spray of water to the ceiling. There was already three inches of water on the floor and it was getting deeper with each passing second.

"What the hell did you do, Kate?"

"Nothing! I swear!" she shouted. "It just happened by itself!"

"The main pipes must have burst and there's no backpressure or something," he breathed heavily.

Then the floor beneath his feet began to shake, the tiles beginning to crack and split. What remained on the shelves shook loose, falling to the floor. Cartons of cigarettes and magazines from behind the counter tumbled to the floor as well. The gas station was falling apart around them.

"They're here!" Tom shouted.

"What do we do… what do we do?" Kate screamed, her eyes wide in terror.

"I don't know, Kate!"

Tom scanned the parking lot of the gas station through the intact front windows, though cracks could be seen on the glass panes. None of the mutant worms had surfaced yet, but they would soon. Maybe they could make it to the car. But where would they go even if they did? Was there really anywhere safe?

The tiles under their feet exploded into shards when a large worm burst up from below. With its orifice wide open, Kate was swallowed up before she could so much as scream. Tom had enough time to lock gazes with her, her eyes pleading for help, then she was gone

"Kate! No"

The worm receded back into its hole, though Tom knew it would be back. Knew it would bring more with it. Patting down his pockets, he pulled out his car keys as tears rolled down his cheeks for the loss of Kate.

He darted outside, racing toward the car. Behind him, Tom could hear the worms crashing through the floor of the station. He didn't look back. He didn't want to see them. He didn't want to be eaten alive like Kate.

He reached the car and yanked open the driver's door. As he turned the key in the ignition, he prayed the battery was fine after the car had sat for a month. The engine whirred once, threatening not to start, but then it roared to life.

"Oh, God. Kate…" Slamming his foot on the gas pedal, he wept harder. "I'm sorry, Kate. I love you."

When he reached the highway, he picked up speed. With the car traveling at nearly eighty-five miles an hour, he kept his eyes locked on the highway.

He drove for what seemed like hours and after a while, his nerves began to settle and he began to think clearly. What was he going to do next? He needed to find other survivors, a safe haven.

He turned on the radio and started flipping through the stations, and to his surprise he found something.

It was faint. The promise of hope and shelter filled his ears, and he was going in the right direction. He had enough gas. He was going to make it!

As his heart filled with hope, the car sped down the road toward the location provided by the radio signal.

The more he listened, he found out it was the people he had been listening to when he'd been on the roof of the gas station. He was saved.

An hour later, the first sign leading him to other survivors was in sight.

Unknown to Tom, the vibrations from his running engine and the tires rolling over the pavement were attracting nearly a thousand worms right to him.

Underground, they followed the car easily, knowing noise meant food.

Inside the car, Tom smiled.

He was safe.

He'd made it.

RIDERS ON THE STORM

NICKOLAS COOK

Stone woke to a cool, bleak, storm-driven morning to find Chelsea missing. He knew the Dogs had taken her because there were blood spots trailing off from camp, like brown little fingerprints of a horrendous crime he and the others had all slept through. He felt an icy lump of dread at the thought of what those mindless monsters had done to her.

He found Preacher curled up in a fetal position and snoring loudly. He kicked him awake with a not so gentle nudge of a steel toed boot. "Wake up, old one. We got trouble." Despite his harsh words, Stone's voice was low and even, not particularly angry, only a numbing acceptance that she was gone.

Probably raped and cut up for breakfast by now.

Preacher was slow to come around and Stone wondered if the old bastard was still hiding a bottle or two behind his back, maybe nipping the hooch at night when everyone else was huddled against the cold and the night. While the old man smacked his cracked, blue-tinged lips and rubbed at crusty eyes, Stone walked the perimeter again.

The single man on watch was, of course, gone too. He'd told them—no, begged them—to keep more than one man on watch at night. But it had been a couple of months since they'd left the Ice Deserts behind and no one had been attacked from an outsider since then, so they'd all, including himself, become complacent, yielding to the natural instinct to live with their guard down, blissfully and ignorantly careless.

And now Chelsea was gone.

They'd have to move again. Out on the desolation roads again to find some new place to crash and wait out the last convulsions of the dying human species.

Across the dead-looking plain of low hills, rocks, and bleached-out weeds, a massive storm was moving slowly from left to right. Even though it was several miles away, he could feel its potential through the ground. It crackled in the air. A vibrational force that tasted of age-old power, created by a nature that didn't give a damn what happened to the pesky little ants called humans. This was an elemental entity that roamed the Earth, blind and omnipotent, a vaporous, electric juggernaut.

Preacher took a long, loud piss and soon wandered to his position a few yards from the still sleeping forms of the others. "Dogs, huh?" The old man smelled ripe and Stone was glad the chill wind was blowing away from him.

"Yeah. Dogs."

Preacher leaned over and blew glistening snot from his nose and sighed in contentment. "Didn't think they moved this far from their usual hunting grounds."

"Me neither."

"Wonder why they didn't do us some serious damage last night?"

Stone shrugged. "Probably a scouting party. Only a couple of them. I found their tracks off over there." He pointed to a dozen yards from the loose circle of sleepers. "Didn't have enough to comfortably take us on." He watched the clouds, bruised blue and purple, roil violently in from the west. "They'll be back tonight, though; probably watching us right now. They'll follow. There'll be a lot more of them this time and they'll attack."

Preacher sniffled and turned to stare at the distance behind them; long miles of hunger and despair to escape what they all knew was certain death. "There's only seven of us left, including you and me. How're we supposed to fight a bunch of bloodthirsty monsters with just that many? Huh? Tell me, Stone. How?" His temper was up, his wrinkled face squirming with fear and rage. "Goddamn it. All this way and their still gonna fucking get us."

Stone kept watching the storm. Eye searing bolts of electricity played throughout the giant, slow-moving formation. "They aren't going to get us, old man. We just need to go where they won't follow."

Preacher stared at him for an unbelieving pause and then followed the other man's icy gaze. "Boy, you are one crazy son-of-a-bitch, ain't ya? Can't wait to see you send that up the flag pole." He walked off, laughing loud enough to wake the remaining sleepers.

Stone had met Preacher six months before, when he and a woman named Helen had been traveling together through a town outside of Omaha, Nebraska. Stone and the old man had taken to one another like lost blood kin. He depended on Preacher's unflinching honesty and will to survive, and he supposed there was something that Preacher found in Stone's icy demeanor as well. In any case, he and the old man had survived some hellish predicaments. They'd seen a lot of people die and yet they continued to walk the line between life and death. There was something to respect in just that, if nothing else.

Now they had joined up with this small band of survivors of the old world, a world of light and reason, which had been brought low by a total failure of modern technology. There were times when Stone could hardly believe how quickly the sane world of order and logic had been ripped asunder by one little misstep of science. A virus…well, to be more accurate, a super virus, had been sent into cyberspace, laying waste to entire systems, some linked, some not. In the end, the Final Solution—as it had come to be known—had been just that: final, and in very dark ways, the solution. No one credible had ever stepped forward to claim responsibility for The Final Solution. Scientists had even theorized no human agent was the cause; that the complex inter-linked systems that stretched across the planet like a vast electronic web may have spontaneously created the virus in response to a perceived threat from mankind. No amount of redundant, million dollar backups, no complicated top of the line super firewalls or security trenches, were able to stop its rapid and inevitable conquest of the world's electronic tools and toys.

It had solved all those nagging problems facing mankind: over population, food shortages, wars. All of those existential issues were like dreams to the ones who remained. Now, the real life problems of continued existence for another day were what plagued them.

Stone, like the others, had once been entrenched in the old world of cell phones, cable TV, broadband wireless service, digital cameras, fast food restaurants, poison in the food, corporate sponsored murder sprees for profit, and government officials abusing power to make for themselves modern versions of fiefdoms. All of that was like someone else's bad dream. What he'd had to face since the surprisingly sudden collapse of the free world economy, and its umbilical cord of hyper-technological dependence, was reality. Harsh, cruel and without mercy. He'd been married, a little girl of his own, a fourteen year veteran police officer for a mid-sized suburban burg, with a little military training to boot.

It had all been ripped away from him in less than a month's time.

Once the ordered society broke down, he lost his wife and child to a group of bloodthirsty raiders who'd come through town with guns and no rules. Sometimes he wondered if they were still alive. Most times he prayed like hell they weren't.

The men who'd taken them had been bad. Some might even call them evil, if one made an effort to believe in such clean delineations ever again.

He sure as hell didn't. Survival was the only rule now.

He would do what must be done to stay alive one more day.

Once Stone got everyone up, he told them about the silent attack that had taken place the night before, about the missing guard and Chelsea. There was a pregnant moment or two of stunned silence before the truth settled down on them like sure doom. Tom Hook was the first one to break the disbelieving quiet. "You don't know they was Dogs that took them," he said, trying in his usual way to take control of the situation. He liked to call it 'playing Devil's advocate,' but in reality Stone knew it was an almost genetic flaw that Hook had to take center stage. He needed attention like dry sand craved rain. "Could've been a roving band of survivors like us. Could be Jeter and that girl done run off together."

Stone fought down the urge to leap at the other man and beat him into the ground, to add his blood to the dried remains of a woman he'd come to care about. "That isn't how it happened," he said instead. "Any man with eyes can check the clues and see what happened."

In the distance, the low rumble of thunder rolled across the open landscape of stunted hills and gray dirt and rock, dried up weeds and grass. The wind grew restless for a moment and blew into their camp with the fierce breath of an ice giant, sending their meager belongings into a timeless dance, fanning the dying embers of their fire.

Mother spoke up. "Tom Hook, would you please be quiet for a change." She pulled the last surviving child of the group—an eight-year-old girl named Abby— close to her breast. "If Stone says it was Dogs that did it, you can bet your sweet caboose that's what happened."

Hook gave an exaggerated roll of his eyes and turned to the others, as if to say: what's one old lady's opinion worth? "All I'm saying is…"

Preacher cut him off. "Is nothing. As usual. Shut your pie hole, boy." He moved off the rock he was sitting on and spit angrily in the dirt. He pointed a stubby, aged finger at Hook. "I walked the perimeter, too. It was Dogs. Make no mistake about it. They left nice clean tracks behind. Four-toed, like always. They don't give a damn if we know it was them or not. In fact, my guess is they want us to know, so we're all good and scared when they come back tonight. And I ain't gotta tell you what'll happen to those of us unlucky enough to survive their attack."

Abby gave a sob and began to squirm in Mother's lap. "They're going to eat me, Mommy."

Mother tried to quiet the frightened child. "Preacher, please."

But Preacher was on a roll now. One scared child didn't matter at the moment. "Woman, don't 'Preacher, please' me," he snapped. "This is damn serious. We all need to know how deep in shit we're in."

"Language, sir!" Mother warned, giving him a stern eye.

"Holy Christ! Language? By God!" the old man roared, throwing his hands into the air dramatically. He turned his face to the sky, as if some hidden gods were privy to this farce of manners versus danger.

Stone jumped in and stopped him with a few carefully chosen words. "We have a chance to get away from them," he said over the old man's rant.

Everyone, including Hook—maybe especially Hook—was suddenly riveted by Stone's low and even voice. "They won't follow us into the storm."

He could feel the slow realization set in on them as to exactly what he was proposing. It was no surprise that Hook was the first to speak again. Stone, for once, was thankful for the other man's naturally dissenting manner. "My God, man! Have you finally lost your ever lovin' mind?" He turned to the others, making sure his voice rang out for all to hear. " 'Into the storm' he says. More like into the jaws of certain death!"

"Jesus Christ Almighty, Hook!" Preacher shouted, slapping his thigh in transports of frustration. "Let the man finish."

Hook looked around at the others for support, but he received only silent stares. Stone had their attention. They'd all seen what the Dogs did to captives; especially the women.

He gazed past Hook, at Chloe and Vern, the husband and wife of the group. They'd lost all three of their children before joining Stone and the others; two of them to roving bands of hungry Dogs. He wanted to make sure they were onboard with his idea. If so, Hook would be completely out voiced and outnumbered, and Stone could then get them all moving as soon as possible. With the storm surging in, daylight hours were going to be severely short today; the sooner they made use of the light, the better their chances of outdistancing the Dogs, who were surely watching them from the distant hills even now. Dogs understood the value of sneak attacks, and the demoralization and divisiveness such attacks caused within a frightened group of people. He almost smiled at the thought of them seeing him and the others running for the storm instead of away from it.

Preacher looked at the others, now so attentive, and then he turned to Stone with a smile. "Whatcha got in mind, Stone?"

Stone laid out the plan, which was simple: gather everything they could carry, load it on their backs, and make a run for the storm.

No one argued. Only Hook mumbled a few words of dissention, but not nearly as loudly as he had before. He knew when his goose was cooked. Preacher was right: they were in deep shit. Running was their only option, and they had to go in the direction the Dogs weren't likely to follow.

Chloe summed up their collective silence best. "Better to be dead in a storm, than to end up in the Dogs' cook pot."

"Or worse," added her husband, as he hugged her close.

Within a half hour, they'd gathered their meager belongings which consisted of ragged clothing, some battered cooking supplies, a scant supply of dried goods scavenged over the long weeks together, a few made or found weapons, such as sharpened spears made of oak wood, a dull rusty bush hook, a cheap samurai sword, various hunting knives, a pitch fork missing its middle tine, three handguns with no ammo, and they were on their way.

Stone took the lead; Preacher limped next to him. The old man's constant nervous chatter was in direct opposition to Stone's cold silence. Stone ignored him and kept turning to watch the hills, waiting for a sign that the Dogs were in pursuit. Their modus operandi had always been night attacks as far as he and the others were aware, but there was no immutable law that said they might not risk a daylight raid if they were pressured into it.

And that's exactly what happened.

The group had not traveled more than a mile before Stone spotted movement to their extreme right, just beyond the low rise of a collection of gray, dry hills. The weeds were sparse in that direction, little more than scraggly top notches in the gray dirt. He wondered why they'd chosen to come in from a direction which provided so little cover. He kept watching them, praying they would stay at the same languid pace.

They were only a mile from the storm. The very air vibrated with electricity. Stone could feel the hairs on his arms and legs standing at attention in the attuned atmosphere. Every breath stank of ozone and death. A chill dampness pervaded the air as well, causing him to shiver with anxiety and cold. Purposely moving into something so vast and powerful was akin to jumping off a cliff with no safety harness. This truly was almost suicidal. The storm was one giant roiling monster of colliding black clouds and angry stabs of eye-searing lightning. The closer they got, the more the cool air hummed with its power and they could see blasted black holes where the lightning had touched down. They could just as easily become one of those deadly black holes in the earth as soon as they entered the storm's circumference. He'd heard strange tales about the things that lived inside those traveling storms. Inhuman things, more demon than human. Creatures of pure energy that lived off the souls of the living. He didn't give them much credence. He was a rational man despite the irrational world he lived in. To believe in storm demons was too much to swallow. Still...the stories got around among the survivors, so many there had to be something to them.

He was staring at the giant bank of shifting black clouds, almost hypnotized by its power. The thick billows of darkness, mixed with deep purple and red bruises, contemplated what insane creature could exist for an extended period within such terrible beauty.

Suddenly, Vern and Hook both gave yells of alarm at the same time.

Several mud-smeared Dogs were swinging in from the left, where the weeds had afforded them more cover. They were less than a quarter mile from the group and closing quickly.

Stone gritted his teeth and cursed silently.

He'd almost fallen for the oldest diversionary trick in the book. While he'd been watching the ones coming from the obvious side, the others had been cautiously sneaking up on them from the side he wasn't watching. Thank God the others had been less concerned with the storm and more attentive to the landscape.

Their cries brought the others to a confused halt, jostling and clanging the few items they had hanging from their bodies.

"What do we do?" Hook cried, his face pale and terrified.

"Run, you damn fool!" Preacher yelled.

His words broke the collective panic that had frozen them in place like frightened deer before approaching hunters, and they began to run in breathless terror for the ever-expanding tempest.

Stone could hear the Dogs howling and crying to one another in their excitement. A quick glance to the left and he could see them running at an angle, hell bent on cutting their prey off from the explosive storm's dubious sanctuary. That gave him an odd sort of hope that safety lay within its path.

He fell back a few feet to make sure everyone was making it. Mother was red-faced and gasping for air, Abby hanging from her neck, bouncing against her aged hip. He snatched the child from her and hurried her along. Abby pressed herself into his neck and sobbed.

Preacher was in the lead, amazingly fast for his age.

Chloe and Vern were holding on to one another's hands, a shared terror in their eyes. They were at the back of the pack. Hook was next to them—only a few feet away from the couple. He looked utterly terrified, like an animal in the slaughter chute.

The Dogs were getting closer to the three of them; Hook seemed to fall back a little more with each passing moment. There was a white panic in his eyes.

Then something happened that would later get under Stone's flesh and make it crawl with uncertainty and repressed rage.

He looked away for an instant to check the progress of the Dogs on the right. He slipped his club from its leather holster, readying it for action.

He heard Vern yell something inarticulate at Hook.

Vern fell, taking Chloe down with him. They crashed and rolled, grunting in surprise and pain as they tumbled head over heel together. Hook looked over his shoulder, less than a yard from them. He kept running and Stone was sure the man was smiling. He hadn't seen what had brought Vern and Chloe down, but there was a nagging doubt already.

That smile burned into his brain. Had Vern fallen…or had he been tripped?

Stone began to turn back, to help his fallen friends, but it was already too late. Their screams grew wild as a group of Dogs fell upon them with a vengeance.

Stone held back his cry of rage and pushed himself, running with all his might. He passed a still smiling Hook and caught up with Preacher.

The storm rose before them like a column of pure malevolence, its boiling clouds like black magic come down to earth. The air was thick with cold violence; a powerful wave of electric potential slammed into them, like an invisible wall of pure energy.

To the right, Dogs were gaining on them, angling in, their sharpened teeth glittering, stained faces aglow with the hope of bloodshed.

Stone waited for them to clutter up nice and tight, jostling one another to be the first to reach the prey. When he thought it was time, he pulled his makeshift club from its swinging holster and gave the heavy weighted wood a twirl or two to build up momentum. At its apex, he released it. The club swung like a deadly boomerang into the grinning, nasty bunch, taking out the leader. His whipcord muscled body went limp and slipped under the others, tangling their legs and arms. They went down as a body, cursing and howling their collective fury as Stone and the others ran the last few feet into the storm's furious safety.

Inside the storm's outer edge, it fell down on them like a vast and weighty curtain of unseen force and energy. Stone had expected pure darkness inside, so he was surprised to find there was quite a bit of ambient light within the storm. It was a pale-green glowing illumination that seemed to come from everywhere and nowhere at once.

The air had a taste like burned aluminum that sat at the back of the throat. A sense of invisible power coursed through it, entered the body, left through the feet, and went back into the earth again. That sense of being like a conduit for this implacable force made him feel small and unimportant, nothing more than a component stuck in the grid.

The wind was much more savage inside, tossing them off balance as they ran, sending them to the ground one moment, pushing them into the air the next. All around, detritus that had been unlucky enough to be caught in the storm's gravitational pull was dancing and flailing through the cold air. Everything from tangles of dead weeds, to arm-thick branches from far away trees that had been in the storm's path, flew through the air with considerable force.

Stone could feel bits of rock and sand pelting him like wasp stings through his jacket. Once, he saw Preacher barely miss having his head taken off by a twisted tree limb that was swinging end over end past him. If the old man had been a little bit slower, he would have been impaled.

The group continued to run until they found a weathered collection of gray and black rocks that stood as tall as the skyscrapers of the old world before the Final Solution. Stone called a rest, told them to get under the largest of the outcrops and seek cover. He put Abby down and the little girl ran to Mother's arms. The old woman held her with a fierceness that belied the fact that they were not blood kin. Already their human conductivity was drawing the lightning down upon them. If they stayed in one place too long, they would be fried, or the storm would pass them by and the Dogs would be waiting. He wasn't sure if the bastards would follow alongside the storm to wait them out, but he wouldn't put anything past them now. Perhaps they would simply take Vern and Chloe as their prizes and leave them alone.

Stone looked over at Hook. He was on all fours, vomiting and sputtering for air.

If he could only be sure…he'd kill the bastard in a heartbeat, no matter what the others might say or think. He'd go it alone if need be. But he wasn't sure. Vern might have fallen. His last cry might have been to tell Hook to keep going. The doubts were too heavy to be ignored simply because he hated Hook. He didn't want to murder a man just for the sake of disliking him.

Preacher was the first to ask, "What happened to Vern and Chloe?"

"Ask Hook," Stone muttered tonelessly. "He was closest to them."

Hook was still recovering, sobbing for air, shaking like one palsied, and could only shake his head incoherently. When he could finally speak, he said simply, "They fell," and offered no further details.

Mother shushed the little girl and turned to Hook. "Why didn't you help them?"

Hook shook his head and silently wiped vomit drool his lips. He didn't look at her or the others.

The storm's fury howled beyond the rocks. A mile away, a huge bolt of lightning ripped across the land, sending blackened rock into the electric thick air. In the brief moment of amplified light, Stone saw something massive and huddled low scurry across the blasted, wind-torn landscape. It looked like a moving rock, but was much faster than could be explained by a terrestrial force moving such a heavy weight. The moment was too brief, however, for Stone to say exactly what he'd seen. He looked around to see if anyone else had seen it, but everyone had their attention on the still gasping Hook.

Another flare of lightning made him wince, but he kept watching the field beyond their cover in the hopes of catching a second glimpse of whatever the thing had been.

If anything, he told himself, it might have been an optical illusion, and if there was any environment that might cause such a thing, this had to be it.

Preacher moved to stand next to Stone. "What did you see, son?" Stone could see the earnestness in his eyes. All Stone had to do was say he'd seen Hook trip Vern and he knew Preacher would lead the way in having Hook barred from the group for good.

But he just wasn't sure, and his sense of ethics, even now a cumbersome thing that nagged quietly at the back of his mind like a know-it-all student in a lecture hall, wouldn't let him tell an untruth.

Still, he would keep a close eye on Hook from here on out. If he was willing to sacrifice part of the group to stay alive, then he was surely going to have some thinking to do when the others figured out that Vern and Chloe had been carrying most of their food supply. By his mental calculations, what they had left wasn't going to last more than a couple of days, at most.

Another huge blast of lightning jumped from the vast and boiling blackness above. It lanced down into the earth a few dozen yards away, ripping the air with its power. Abby's screams could barely be heard over the explosion. Stone squinted against the light, and for a fraction of a second, was sure he saw another of those huddled masses moving across the field and towards the smoking hole. Then the dimness fell again and he wasn't sure if it had been real or not. No one else spoke up, so he stayed quiet. No sense in scaring them anymore than they already were.

Once they were calmer, he laid out their options. Yes, they were safe enough for the time being, but soon the storm would move past them, and if the Dogs were still outside the storm, they'd descend upon them with a vengeance. They could follow the storm, but of course there were the dangers of being zapped by lightning, or speared by an errant tree limb. And there was no guarantee that the Dogs would be waiting for them when they finally came out again.

They were quiet, only Abby whimpering when the lightning blossomed outside their makeshift cover.

Mother was the first to offer a suggestion. "Perhaps we could move away from them, go to the other side of the storm altogether."

"We ain't got any idea how far that might be," Preacher said. "For all we know, this damn thing could be a hundred miles wide."

Mother gave him a disbelieving smirk. "Surely, that's ridiculous."

"A hundred miles might be a conservative estimate, Mother," Stone said. "I've heard tales that some of these things can stretch from one end of the state to the other." After a moment's hesitation, he added, "Besides, we wouldn't have enough food to chance a crossing."

The truth dawned on them slowly, but firmly. Stone glanced at Hook, but his face betrayed nothing, which only fed Stone's doubts about the man's guilt.

"So I leave it up to you how we should carry on from here," Stone said, taking them in with his hard eyes, each in turn.

"Well, the way I see it," Preacher said after a moment of scratching his gray beard in consideration. "The Dogs don't have no better idea of what we're gonna do than we do about their plans. Seems to me it's a fifty-fifty chance, right?"

"Not really," Stone replied. "They got a lot more numbers than us. There's nothing to say they haven't already stationed some of their warriors where we entered and sent more ahead in case we try to escape them that way."

"We could run back the way we came," Mother said. "Double back on them."

"If we think of it, then they could, too." Everyone looked at Hook. His voice was thick with terror. They all felt his emotions rising like the winds around them. His hands shook and his face was drawn tight and thin.

"Then what the hell do we do?" Preacher threw his hands into the air in frustration.

Stone waited for the old man to sit again. "I say we go forward. Going backwards means we have to face them again on their home turf. If we move onward for a good spell, we might outrun them or outthink them. I don't know, but it seems to me the best chance we have."

"But this storm…" Hook began, cowering fearfully as another stroke of bright lightning bit into the ground less than a quarter mile away.

"The Dogs are a sure death," Stone said. "We might make it through the storm."

"It's worth a shot," Preacher agreed.

Mother nodded, hugging the little girl closer. Hook slumped down, hiding his face in his hands as the ground shook under the storm's violence.

"Then it's settled," Stone said. "The sooner we do it, the better."

After a small drink of water each, they gathered their courage and moved out into the fury of the storm again. It was hard to believe that less than a few hundred yards away it was still daylight and the world was relatively sane. While inside this hellish maelstrom nothing seemed to sit still for more than a moment or two, tossed and buffeted by the incredible implacable winds.

As they huddled together and began a slow run forward, the wind's ferocity seemed to increase, and Mother, the smallest of the adults, could barely make headway, despite Abby's added weight. Stone saw her difficulty, and without a word, got behind her and used his own body to help move her forward.

It was slow going, but soon the wind fell away to less than hurricane strength for a bit and she was able to move on her own. Preacher jogged on Stone's left, Hook on his right. They had gone perhaps no more than a mile, dodging the larger bits of detritus, cowering, when the lightning struck nearby.

Stone heard a muffled yell and then Preacher was gone. His body was swept away by something large as a car. Stone fell to the ground, pulling Mother and the little girl down with him. Something flew over their heads, a shadowy, twisting form that disappeared into the darkness behind them before he could make it out.

Mother was screaming something at him, but Stone couldn't hear her over the banshee winds. Sand blasted at his face. He could feel dampness the wind chased down his cheeks that was either tears or blood. He didn't bother to wipe it away to find out which it was. Mother was still screaming and Stone realized in horror that her arms were empty. Abby was gone.

He twisted his body around, putting his straining back to the force of the wind, peering into the darkness beyond. Lightning burst upon the landscape, turning the enforced night into surrealistic day. A large metal object, beaten and rusted, lay a little ways from them. In the all too brief moment of illumination, Stone could see an arm sticking from under the wrecked machine.

Giving a sobbing Mother the signal to stay down and remain still, Stone started to crawl towards it, afraid to stand up. Hook was still cowering on the ground a few feet from Mother, unwilling or unable to move. Stone left him there. The ground was like dusty stone, hard and gritty, blown to a smooth finish by the deadly winds.

Something hit him in the back and he felt a white hot pain where it struck, but he kept focus on the arm under the torn-apart car. As he neared, he could see it was a small arm, not a wrinkled one. He knew without going further that it was Abby. He had to make sure she was dead. If she had a chance to survive, he wouldn't turn his back on her, though he knew in his heart that she was better off dead. No child should have to live in a hell of godlike storms and flesh-eating cannibals, of roving bands of insane gun-toting soldiers and blood-thirsty rabid animals.

He made it to the car, pulling himself up by its rickety front fender. It had once been white, but time and the elements had turned it a dried blood rust color, leaving only a few patches of original paint here and there.

The windshield had long ago been smashed out, and the interior rotted away or stolen for some practical purpose or other, leaving the beaten hull behind. The wind must have entered it just right at some point and lifted it into the air for a journey across God only knew how far. It had come here, just in time to crush a little girl who had done nothing but be born in the wrong place at the wrong time. Only a few years before, she would have lived a full and happy life. Now she was crushed under a half ton of uncaring metal.

He pulled himself forward a few more inches, until he could peer at the other side of the twisted metal. His breath froze in his throat. Preacher's head had been burst open like a pulped piece of red and gray fruit, his body beneath half of a dented, sharpened fender cusp.

His friend was dead.

Stone wanted to kick the car, punch in the dented hood. He wanted to hurt the unthinking, uncaring thing that would kill his only true friend in such a degrading manner. Instead, he moved inside the car, trying to find a way to get at Abby, so he could at least pull her out, find some way to give her a proper burial.

Preacher was a lost cause; the old one was too deeply buried beneath a half ton of metal to recover. Stone's hands gripped the jagged metal, holding on for dear life as the wind suddenly rose again, tearing through the interior, throwing him against the crushed dashboard and twisted steering column. His head smashed against something hard and unforgiving, then he saw only darkness.

He dreamed.

In his dream, he was flying and the land below was all in darkness, punctuated sporadically by bright painful light, then back into molasses-thick night again.

He was tumbling head over heels, and he thought about an old movie he'd seen as a kid, *The Wizard of Oz,* and Stone realized with an ironic smirk that he'd become the girl swept away to a far away land by the power of a sinister storm.

An angry red light brightened to the point of pain and he couldn't move away from its power. The searing crimson light found his most secret terrors and forced them out of hiding like a giant fist squeezing blood from a rock. Stone screamed but no one heard him. An overwhelming ambient noise, like a furious down-pour carried his wails into oblivion.

He awoke to Mother's screams. At first he thought it was only the wind, as it ripped through the rocking hunk of a metal shell where he lay curled up in the fetal position at the bottom, jammed against the twisted seat. But no wind ever held such a note of pure animal terror.

Slowly and painfully, he managed to pull himself into a rough sitting position to peer outside into the blue light of the raging storm. Mother was being bore down by two of the hulking shapes he'd seen before, one on each side of her, pulling her away.

Hook was nowhere to be seen.

Stone dragged himself clear of the car, fighting the wind and the rusty movements of the devastated vehicle, until he fell the last few feet to the ground in a moaning heap. He tried to steady himself and ran clumsily towards Mother and her two rock-like attackers. He drew his only weapon left—a dull-looking army knife hidden in the folds of his clothing.

Mother's screams were louder as she realized how strong her attackers were. Stone gave a low growl, and hit the one on the left from behind with his shoulder at ramming speed. The cloaked figure crumpled under the attack and he swung unsteadily around to face the other one.

There was no face inside the cloak, only blackness and two shining eyes that looked as cold and inhuman as two insect cara-paces side by side. But something did live within that darkness. It swiped at a stunned Stone, hitting him in the chin, sending Stone flying back with the force of the unexpected blow.

Then it immediately turned its attention back to Mother, as if Stone was nothing more than an insignificant gnat buzzing in the storm.

Mother's screams escalated; more violent and insane sounding.

Stone shook his head, trying to clear his muddled thoughts, still gripping the knife in his hand. He tried to gain his feet again, but an errant branch flew from the blue dimness and hit him in the back. He sprawled forward, seeing black stars circle his peripheral vision.

When he was able to get control of himself, Mother's screams had faded into blurry moans under the yowls of the wind. The other cloaked being was gone as well. Stone dug his hands into the dry ground and pulled himself to his feet. He had to find Mother.

She had to still be alive. She was the only one left. All those people he'd come to care for as a new family, people with which he'd broken bread, fought with, cried with, slept in huddled fearful piles, were all dead or missing. Except for Mother. He wasn't going to let her die. No matter what those things were, he was going to save her.

It took only a few moments to narrow down where they had taken her: a black hole gaped in the earth not far from where he'd last seen her being dragged away. He staggered to it, wary of more flying debris intent on taking him to the ground, until he knelt at the edge of the hole. It looked deep, emitting no ambient light.

Stone put the knife in his teeth like the literary pirates of old and dove in headfirst. There was no fear in him now. Death would have been a relief after all he'd seen and been through, all he'd lost since the virus came to destroy his world.

He slid along a cold, relatively smooth surface, big enough to allow him easy entrance, although he could feel the curved walls to either side if he held out his hands. Once inside, the fury of the storm died away to a grumbling mutter, and he became aware of the sound of his heaving breath.

There was a smell, too. Oily and alien, inhuman, beneath that same electric ozone stink he'd felt inside the storm. Something about the improbable stink made the small hairs on his arms stand at attention, a preternatural warning of impending danger, perhaps, or an animal response to the profane. That black face with the shining eyes sat heavy on his soul as he pulled himself faster into whatever ending the tunnel held for him.

It ceased abruptly with a solid thump as he fell a few feet onto a smooth surface which felt like cold rock that had been buffed by unknown hands. He pulled the knife from his teeth and waited a moment, feeling his blood pump through his burning veins.

A woman's muffled scream came from the right.

Stone moved cautiously and uncertainly towards where he thought the sound had emanated. Then he heard a man's agonized screams come from the same direction. He gave up caution and hurried towards the sounds.

A tinge of azure appeared to his right, pushing back the otherwise space deep blackness. He controlled his breathing as best he could and rounded the corner of smooth gray rock to see what lay beyond.

The horror of the sight before him froze him in his steps. The infernal scene was lit by a dim electric blue light that seemed to emanate from the collective of huddled cloaked figures.

A band of the cloaked, faceless beings with shiny eyes were gathered around two wooden crosses in the middle of the room. There was a strangely religious tone to the scene. Mother was hanging upside down from one of the crosses, and Hook was hanging from the other. Both had been stripped of their ragged and soiled clothing, and were naked to the cold emotionless eyes of the silent horde. Every few moments, one or both of them would scream out in anguish as one of the cloaked beings stepped forward and peeled a strip of flesh off them.

Hook looked red and glistening in the warm firelight. His eyes were two blazing balls of insanity, peering from the undone mold of his face. His nose was missing; there were only two blood-spouting holes that blew gore each time he exhaled, like a whale blowing water from its hole when it surfaces.

Mother was being quickly dismantled as another of the things slipped from the utterly silent, milling crowd and used its silvery, ethereal looking hands to pull away a strip of skin from her left ribcage. The old woman screamed like a frightened animal, her wails echoing throughout the rock chamber.

Stone's first gut instinct was to turn and run, but he remembered the repugnance and fury he'd felt when he'd suspected Hook of purposely sacrificing two of their makeshift family of survivors to save his own hide. He would not—could not—do the same, even if it seemed to him his comrades were a lost cause. With every passing moment, more blood splashed to the stone floor, more torture, and less of the two that was recognizable as living, thinking beings.

Another of the figures seemed to elongate towards them from the weird collective and it reached forward in a flash and took a swipe at Hook's shivering, dangling form. His body gave an involuntary convulsion as the shimmering, writhing hand tore away the flesh from his upper left thigh. Hook was seemingly beyond the influence of physical pain now; there was only a momentary flash in his eyes which displayed his waning awareness.

Stone, for the first time, paid attention to what the obviously inhuman creature did with its gory prize. That strangely unstable hand looked as if it engulfed the dripping bit of Hook and then it was gone. The creature stepped back, still silent, and tilted its head, as if digesting Hook's stolen flesh on more than one level. For a moment that oily, machine-like ozone stench flared in the chamber, then wafted away. Stone realized he'd been unconsciously picking up that scent every time the things took a bite of the half-dead humans for consumption. He shook his head in confusion

What the hell were they?

Black phantom faces, shining insectile eyes, inhuman movement without visible bipedal propulsion, and hands that seemed to be made up of millions of loosely connected silvery black dots that swarmed in a weirdly universal pattern. He had never heard of anything before, or after the Final Solution to explain these creatures.

Stone might have crouched indefinitely in the shadows of the entrance to the chamber—frozen in horrified perplexity—had not Mother's wide, crazed eyes found him there, cowering and afraid. The old woman's mouth formed a crimson welt and let loose with a terrible alarm of recognition, or pleading, or perhaps both.

The creatures turned in their strange floating manner as one organism to find him, knife in hand, teeth bared in a rictus of horror. And then, as one, they swarmed at him.

Stone forgot all fits of self-loathing and backed away, turning to run. The creatures moved like flying things, cloaks flapping in the oily stillness, impelled by some mysterious engine within.

He tripped over a rock the size of his head, and went tumbling down. The knife dropped from his hands, disappeared in the dimness beyond the blue light of the chamber. The first of the beings was upon him, its scintillating hands reaching to flay his skin like the others.

Stone frantically grabbed for anything to defend himself, couldn't locate the knife, but did find the rock he'd tripped over. Grasping it, he hurled the rock into the looming, hooded head. For a moment, as the rock made impact, he caught a terrifying glimpse of its carapace eyes, glittering from within, then the rock crushed what lay within the cloak. The hood flew into millions of individual pieces, scattering into a static-charged cloud of black and silver dots and bright blue sparks, then the rock thumped to the ground behind the creature. The now hoodless, headless, eyeless thing's hands made an automatic gesture to restore order in its dissipated body part, but then they also blew apart into two smaller clouds of flashing electricity. The entire body crumpled at Stone's feet and the cloak began to writhe, as if beneath it a colony of ants crawled about. The cloak was subsumed by the writhing motion and became transparent, then disappeared.

Stone was sure his eyes were mistaken, that the fault lay in the thick shadows and too little light, and helped by his extreme terror, he didn't want to admit to seeing those silvery blobs with tiny bits of assimilated human flesh swimming within the liquid mess at his feet.

Instead, he jerked himself to stand and ran for where he thought the tunnel must be. But he must have become turned around because, soon, he knew, even in his panicked state, that he'd easily gone three times the distance he traveled to reach the chamber the first time. All was pure black, and only his frightened, gasping breaths and the painful thumps of his hands on the smooth walls to either side came to him. He stumbled through the passage, trusting he'd find either life or death sooner or later. After a time, he smelled dampness.

Rain water.

The dim sound of the raging tempest outside the cave became louder, overwhelming the sound of his terror. Then he could see the walls again. There was a dim, ambient glow from the storm's electric potential.

The walls gave way before him in a sudden recession of darkness and he was thrust into the storm once more. Stone kept running, heedless now of the flying debris, driven by near hurricane force winds, that could send a sharpened tree branch, or a piece of rusty metal, through him like a hurled spear from an invisible foe. He ran, head down, sucking in the cold, ozone heavy air, sobbing uncontrollably. He had no track to guide him, only where his flagging strength would carry him. Eventually, that gave out and he collapsed to the ground. Giant flares of lightning leaped across the tumultuous sky, and thunder ripped across the landscape of the circling storm.

He awoke in the car again, unsure what was reality and what was a nightmare. Now it was daylight and the storm had passed him by. It was cool and wet. Spent raindrops dripped from the rusting shell of the car. A breeze blew inside.

Preacher was impossibly squatting near him, seemingly asleep. The old man's face was a ruin of dried blood and muddy stains.

He wasn't dead.

Stone could hear his slow, even breathing.

He didn't understand. He had been sure the car had crushed his friend. While he was trying to work out how he could have been mistaken, he fell asleep again.

This time, when he opened his eyes, Preacher was awake and watching him. They looked at each other across the half-torn car for a long stretch of uncertain silence.

"You live," the old man said.

Stone thought Preacher's voice sounded muddy and thick, unlike before the events of the storm.

Stone cleared his throat, and managed to croak, "So it seems." He smiled, but Preacher didn't return it. "I thought you were dead, crushed by the car, old one." Preacher's eyes stared coldly back at him. Stone felt his strange disquiet grow.

This wasn't Preacher.

That icy wave of realization galvanized him. Stone looked for something to use as a weapon. There! A rusted hunk of metal flange from the car's interior. He reached for it, but the thing that was not Preacher lunged for it as well, his arm elongating to an impossible length. In a flash, he held the makeshift weapon in his wrinkled, writhing hand.

Stone froze, waiting to feel the killing blow.

But it didn't come.

Instead, the false Preacher tossed the weapon from the car, then turned to stare at Stone again with its implacable, alien eyes. There was a discernible sheen to them that wasn't human. Insect-like. Like the creatures in the cave that had taken Mother and Hook. That had, of course, taken Preacher, his friend.

The thing sat back down.

After a time, Stone said, "What are you going to do to me?" His weariness was bone deep, and he almost didn't care what happened anymore. He'd seen too much. His emotions were worn into rotting threads, ready to release him into a thankful oblivion of insanity, then death.

"You will guide me," Preacher said. "I have been sent forth to find the Creators."

"Creators?" Stone watched with disgust at the unnerving manner in which the old man's flesh seemed to crawl in little fits and starts, as if the things that made it up were uncertain of their correct order in the complicated framework which they had usurped.

Preacher cocked his head. "The father. The mother. The Creators. We must find them. We have a message to deliver."

Despite the terror at the thing before him, Stone couldn't help but give it a derisive smirk. "Friend, you're way too late to find anyone that even cares what message you might have to give. Let alone any father or mother. Your Creators are all fucking dead, destroyed by their own pride and greed."

The Preacher thing eyed Stone for a silent moment, thinking for a time. While it did, its neck and face swam in waves across the old man's features. Stone grimaced in distaste, trying not to think about his lost comrade.

It said, "We must deliver the message. You will guide me."

"Fuck you."

"You will." It sounded so sure of itself that Stone had to fight to keep from leaping the distance to ram his fists against its cold, inhuman face.

"There's nothing left," Stone snapped. "Don't you get it?"

"You will guide me."

He stared wearily at the thing's writhing features. The Preacher thing's shining beetle wing eyes stared back without emotion or concern.

They sat silently until the cool breeze disappeared and the sun began to heat the metal frame of the car around them. Stone felt like he was being cooked slowly by the heat of the unforgiving sun.

Finally, he stooped over and began to crawl from the car's interior. Preacher followed, flowing like silver liquid to the ground. He reached back with a long arm and drew forth Stone's old backpack.

Stone could hear water sloshing around in his canteen inside the pack. Bulges of food could be seen.

They stood side by side, silent, a slight reminder of the morning breeze playing through Stone's sweat-dampened hair.

"Which way," Stone asked, looking at his inhuman companion.

Preacher pointed west with his shimmering, writhing silver finger. Blue sparks leaped between each finger.

Without a word, Stone began to walk in that direction. The Preacher thing followed in his wake, stumbling slightly, as it still learned to walk like a human being.

DANGEROUS PETS

VINCENZO BILOF

Hubert was pleased he was going to get to spend some time out of his cage, knowing he was lucky to be let out at all. Hubert was an abomination of the worst kind, and by all rights, should have been killed and burned the moment he'd emerged from his mother's cursed womb.

Hubert eagerly leapt out of his cage and landed in a pile of straw that was strewn about the hut. His family was wealthy enough to keep him in his own shelter; most other families that owned a pet usually left the cages outside to the mercy of the elements. Most pets didn't live very long after purchase, and they were mostly a luxury for wealthy families to enjoy for a brief period of time.

"Human shit." Hubert was kicked in the back by the large-footed Vesuvius. As Hubert tumbled into the bright sunlight, he could hear Vesuvius laughing along with his small contingent of his close friends.

Vesuvius was taller than most Naga. His black-scaled skin made him seem an obelisk carved out of obsidian in the glare of the wrathful summer sun. At eight feet tall, Vesuvius was the star of his generation. A young man with several successful hunts under his belt, he carried with him a large broadsword that had been crafted especially for him—another luxury a wealthy family enjoyed. He wore a necklace of human fingers around his neck, and his leather pants and shirt had been cured and tanned from his human victims.

Hubert always felt that humans bore a fairly close resemblance to their superiors. Save for the black, scaly flesh that served as a guard against the Earth's merciless sun, the Naga were simply one evolutionary leap above the meek humans that sparsely populated the world within hunting reservoirs. The Naga had sparse white hair atop their skulls, and because their skin had adapted to the irradiated world, they didn't need to wear anything on their feet.

Vesuvius was the perfect Naga specimen, an example of why humans had become obsolete after the Fire God had eradicated most of the species.

"Had him since he was a pup," Vesuvius pointed at Hubert with a long, curled fingernail, his luminescent green eyes set like gems within his coal-black face. "Hubert, I want to show my friends how you play. You'll make me proud that I own you."

Vesuvius motioned for Hubert to stand, "Shit-boy, stand up and put your neck in this collar. If you behave, I might let you eat from one of my own kills from this afternoon's hunt."

Hubert did as he was told. He was careful not to let any of his tangled, brown hair get within the manacle's cold iron.

Vesuvius dragged his human pet across the ruins of the charred metropolis that was home to nearly a thousand Naga, which was a large group, considering that only a few scattered pockets of Naga had managed to survive the Agony, which was something that Hubert often heard mentioned, though he was hardly familiar with it. Human pets and captives were kept in cages and it was forbidden for any of them to not be accompanied by their masters.

"He's really going to do it?" one of the other Naga ribbed Vesuvius.

"Of course. He loves to play." Vesuvius crouched down and rubbed his clawed hand through Hubert's hair. "He's so incredibly loyal to me. I couldn't ask for a better companion. He lets me cut him whenever I want. I haven't grown bored with him—yet. Soon though, I think I'll have his left arm. There's not a lot of meat on it. I'd hate to waste a good pet, but I'll grow out of him, soon."

Hubert shuddered. Vesuvius traced his fingernail along one of the many scars that adorned Hubert's thigh.

"Don't let me or my friends down," Vesuvius said through his teeth. "I brought the girls home just for you to enjoy. Humans are soft, and hardly any fun to hunt, now. Do you know, Hubert, how many screaming beasts tasted my steel today? I swam in a river of blood, shit-boy. Doesn't that make you happy?"

Hubert nodded quickly. He would do whatever it took to please his master.

The human females were young, their faces stained with tears. Hubert had never seen living, human girls before, and he glanced up at his master helplessly. He knew what he was going to be asked to do, because he'd done it before on males. One female was a brunette, the other an ashen-blond.

They were helplessly chained to a lamppost as dust kicked up into their faces from a sudden gust of wind. Iron collars were clamped around their necks. Their skin was sunburned, their eyes wide with fear.

"He can be like us," Vesuvius said, pointing to Hubert. "You're all nothing more than meat. My pet has been well-trained, because he's an animal, like you. He'll do what I tell him."

"Fucking mutant!" one of the girls spat at Vesuvius.

The monstrous warrior laughed, his friends doing the same. He produced a tiny shard of broken glass and handed it to Hubert.

"Choose," he told his pet. "The other female must watch. Show them what kind of animals they really are."

Hubert stared at the shard of glass in his shaking fist. The blond-haired girl continued to whimper meekly, while the brunette, who'd spat at Vesuvius, stared up at him with defiant eyes.

One of Vesuvius' friends said, "He's not gonna do it!"

Vesuvius gently placed a hand on Hubert's shoulder. "He will do it. He likes to please me. Besides, he's never seen human females before. He's more than twenty years old... he might be feeling a bit lonely at the moment."

The others laughed.

The sun temporarily faded behind cloud cover, and a shadow descended upon the ghostly ruins of crumbled masonry and skeletal automobiles. Hubert knelt beside the whimpering girl. She howled in terror as Hubert, a malnourished, ragged slave-boy, brushed a lock of hair away from her face. He wanted to look into her eyes, but she squeezed them closed. She desperately kicked, and Hubert tilted his head and watched her useless protests.

Surely, her life had been one of suffering and fear. Her family had likely been killed already by Vesuvius or other Naga, and she'd spent most of her life fleeing from the painful death that awaited her eventually. Pleasure and peace were strangers to her during her short life.

"This will be the last thing that you feel," Hubert whispered softly.

While the defiant brunette shouted obscenities at Hubert, Vesuvius seized her to make sure she wouldn't interrupt the show. Though she was chained, Hubert was within reach of her legs. With each cut, the blond girl writhed in pain. Hubert had been forced to kill human males for the pleasure of his master on numerous occasions, but those had been relatively quick ordeals. Hubert wanted to know how much he could make the girl actually feel. How long would it be before she finally died? How would she die? Shock? Blood loss? He was excited at the possibilities. What would please Vesuvius the most?

If he was able to please his master, then he might be allowed an evening out of his cage. That freedom was worth the blood on his hands.

As the glass shard ripped into the girl's flesh, Hubert studiously observed the blood that welled up from the wound he was carving in her upper thigh. He held her by the throat with one hand, though his attempt to steady her while he worked was barely enough to keep her from twisting, his cutting becoming erratic. He hoped to complete the process without removing the shard, but was forced to start over numerous times.

His leg was pressed to the ground, and it was soon immersed in a pool of blood by the time he finished with his first chunk of flesh. Hubert looked up into Vesuvius' green eyes, and his master nodded in approval. Hubert shoved the chunk into his mouth and chewed.

When the blond girl was finally dead, Hubert, now covered in gore, admired his handiwork. The furious brunette had stopped resisting midway through the process. She had offered words of comfort to the dying girl, even calling her name, though Hubert hadn't been able to hear it over his victim's screams.

As early evening began to fall upon the dead city, Vesuvius announced, "Let this one stay out here overnight. Everyone knows she's my property. I might keep her as a pet to reward Hubert, or I might eat her brain. I need to think about it. She's rather spunky, after all." Vesuvius ruffled Hubert's hair. The slave grinned.

That evening, the Naga partied in the ruins. Their black-scaled flesh glistened in the torchlight, and human blood ran over their lips from prey that had been collected during the day's hunt, to be removed from cages and cooked over a roaring fire pit.

Hubert was allowed the freedom to roam around and watch the festivities take place. The Naga would sometimes allow their pets such freedom, considering that there wasn't any likelihood they would be able to live in the wild on their own. Hubert understood that he wouldn't fit in with humans—proof of this was the blond girl's reaction when he'd cut into her. After all, he'd told her it was best for her to savor the moment.

Hubert had been the accidental offspring of a human female and a Naga. Such was forbidden under Naga law because the humans were considered uncivilized creatures. Humans belonged in the wild. As Hubert had heard the tale, the Naga was executed along with his mother. Hubert was initially kept alive because the Naga were curious to see if he would undergo the Agony—whatever that was. As the years passed, he was trained to serve as the perfect plaything for Vesuvius, who was being groomed for a seat on the city council. One day, Vesuvius was going to lead his own hunting parties.

While Hubert wanted to understand the human threshold for all sensations, he often wondered when his own death would occur. Surely, he would be honored if his master was the one who ate his flesh. Many times, a revered pet would be eaten by its master as a toast to an enduring friendship. Most pets, however, were left to die in the sun.

What would happen if the other girl escaped? he wondered. Could she lead Hubert to a human sanctuary out in the wild, if he spared her life? Would she pity him enough to show him where more humans were hiding?

Vesuvius would be proud of him if he took the initiative.

There was also a part of him that wondered what it might be like to live among his own kind. How did the savages live? Could he adapt to their way of life? Would it mean... freedom? Hubert felt a strange, uncomfortable longing to see her again.

In the abyssal gloom of night that enveloped the ruins, it was impossible to see Vesuvius standing over him, though Hubert wasn't caught off-guard. He could *feel* his master's presence after years of living as a cherished pet.

"You've made me very proud, shit-boy," Vesuvius said. A cracking flame from a nearby torch provided enough light for Hubert to see the scales on his master's black flesh. "You've been chosen to partake in the Agony. You're coming with me now to witness how it takes place, and you'll be rewarded with the knowledge of our proud race."

Hubert beamed. He'd never seen Vesuvius acknowledge him with any form of respect before, and he felt honored and incredibly special. He felt as if he was finally gaining some measure of acceptance among the Naga. Would they consider him an equal after the Agony?

Hubert cautiously approached a massive steel drum, which was located in the center of a Naga circle. Hubert's heavily scarred body drew whispers and glances from those in attendance, and Vesuvius placed a hand on his slave's shoulder to demonstrate that the human was his property.

A skinny, older human male slave rested at the feet of the Naga that Hubert immediately recognized as the city's chief praetor. Beowulf was the most renowned warrior that had ever hunted for human flesh, and he was also Vesuvius' father. His nearly white hair was a flowing mane over his shoulders, marking him as a second-generation Naga. The hair, apparently, thinned as the bloodlines thinned.

Hubert could see a thick, green liquid was inside the drum.

Beowulf addressed the circle around him, sweeping his hand over the crowd as he began his sermon. "It was our prophet who dreamt of us, and we are here because of him. It was our prophet who dreamed that a superior race could live in this world, but before his dream could be realized, he asked the Fire God for the Great Cleansing. The bombs fell from the heavens, and our world was purged of the taint of mankind.

"Thus began the Agony. Many of the humans who survived breathed in the very gift that would begin the first step in the evolution of a superior race. Yes, the Naga are descended from those soft, week humans. The skin began to change, and those who suffered and endured the transformation experienced the Agony, and thus, the Naga were born."

Hubert couldn't help but wonder if he was actually going to become a Naga soon. How could it be possible?

"Our skin can endure any climate, and it never wrinkles or grows brittle with our bones as we age. The Naga cannot die—we are eternal! The humans feared us and sought to destroy us, but we defended ourselves and acquired a taste for their precious flesh."

Beowulf lifted the slave to his feet, as he'd been kneeling next to him on the cracked pavement.

"There are humans among us who've earned, through their loyalty, an opportunity to become one of us," he continued. "To become Naga. Of course, no human has ever survived the Agony since the first generation was born."

Hubert was beginning to suspect what was happening, though he didn't want to admit it to himself. He felt as if his master was going to betray him. Hubert had earned his share of brutal punishments, and would gladly take another, but Vesuvius had said he was going to be honored with something special.

Beowulf lifted the skinny slave off the ground and turned him upside-down.

"I'm free! I'm finally free! I had a family once!" the skinny slave cried out. The man was dipped headfirst into the green liquid. His body twitched in Beowulf's grasp until the praetor lifted him out. The dark green liquid steamed as it dripped from his face, arms, and chest.

"Linda! My mate's name was Linda!" the skinny slave gurgled. "I've said it again, after all this time!"

Beowulf's brow furrowed. He dipped the man again and held him for a longer time. The Naga in the circle began to stand and make bets on how long the man would live, and still others made bets that the man would survive and begin to transform.

Bubbles emerged along the surface of the green fluid, and in the faint light that the torches provided, Hubert could see that that a darker substance began to mix in with the green. Naga began to clap their hands and pat each other on the back.

A cold shiver ran down Hubert's spine.

The bloody, smoking mess Beowulf lifted out of the drum hardly resembled anything that might once have been human. More cheers went up through the crowd, and Beowulf held the dead slave high for everyone to see. Teeth fell out of the sagging jaw as the eyes slowly melted away. Flesh sluiced off the bulbous skull and body of the sacrificed man.

"You're going to be the first to transform," Vesuvius said in Hubert's ear. "If you disappoint me, you will die."

Hubert understood that Vesuvius had nothing to lose: he already had a replacement in mind after Hubert's moment with the Agony.

Hubert found out he was going to have his own opportunity to experience the Agony after the next hunt. While he understood that death for a human was inevitable, he didn't want to be replaced by another slave.

His feelings on the matter were conflicted: he could certainly please his master by surviving the Agony, or he could die. Either way, it would all be in service to the Naga that owned him. It was part of his duty to die whenever his master decided it should happen.

But Vesuvius decided that the female human, the captive brunette who'd been forced to watch Hubert kill the blond girl, would replace *him*.

There might be an opportunity for Hubert to escape from the Naga, to live among the humans, to satisfy the primal urge that nagged him whenever he thought about the girl.

While the celebration continued long into the night, he tried to come up with a plan. Surely, the girl would take him with her when he freed her. He had no doubt about that. She would pity him and take him to a human encampment, where they would try to show him how to live. If he couldn't live there, he could always come back to Vesuvius. He would have fresh information on the human outpost and would explain that he simply acted for the benefit of the Naga.

Vesuvius would have the key to the girl's collar. He would often lock humans up in random sections of the city and leave them to burn in the sunlight simply to demonstrate his superiority over them. All Naga loved to show how much more different—and thus more powerful they were—than humans.

He waited until his master predictably sought the companionship of a female Naga during the party. Vesuvius had both the power and prestige to pick only the finest women, and sometimes, he chose more than one. Hubert wondered if human males were allowed the same comforts in their own society.

His master secured the privacy for his tryst behind the silent, foreboding ruins of a sprawling structure that could have seated several thousand people within it when humans had ruled the world. Hubert always wondered what kinds of spectacles would take place in such a massive structure that had been reduced to cold, fire-blackened brick and twisted steel.

Hubert rummaged through his master's discarded garments for the key, then crept into the deep shadows, where grunting and sudden gasps were close enough for him to nearly lose his resolve. What if Vesuvius saw him? The smell of Naga sweat made him think what it might be like for humans to enjoy similar pleasures—he thought of the chained girl he was going to rescue.

Thankfully, he was right. Vesuvius had the key with him. Elated by his discovery, he had to remind himself that he still had to be careful and quick. He had to duck his head to avoid the human bones that were thrown at him by other Naga, while he made his way past the barrage of insults. He scampered over the ruins toward the girl. Picking his way through the wreckage, he hoped his memory wouldn't fail him, and that she was still alive.

He was really going through with it. He was going to escape.

Hubert nearly tripped over the girl in the dark. In the scant light provided by the glaring, white moon above, he saw a dark stain on the cement where the blond girl that he'd carved up had died.

The brunette seemed a ghastly, cold corpse, her black wispy hair covering her face. She stood and jangled her chain. "You!" she spat in Hubert's face.

He shook his head. "No, no, no. See, I've come to help you."

"You can't even help yourself," she said venomously. "You're nothing but a Naga pet. We've seen the likes of you in our villages. They send you in like dogs, and they expect us to take you in, to help you. But you're all the same."

Hubert quickly shook his head. "I have a key. I want to come with you. I want to leave."

"You enjoyed what you did, didn't you? You didn't just do it because that Naga bastard told you to. You don't deserve to live; do you know that? She was a good person, and you tortured her. You made her watch as you stuffed parts of her in your mouth. You should have let that Naga kill you, then and there. I bet you've done it before, too."

Hubert could feel that his situation was becoming desperate. He'd already gone too far, and even if Vesuvius didn't already know the key was missing, it would be difficult for Hubert to return it. More than anything, he wanted to reach out and grab a fistful of her hair. He could hurt her, of course, but his need for her seemed to control his actions. He didn't know what to do with her to make the feeling stop, but he knew she would have to be freed.

"I want to leave," he said. "See, I have the key." He tried to show it to her in the darkness. "You don't understand what the Naga can do. My master—Vesuvius—he could have made me beg for death. You must help me."

"Unlock me," she commanded.

He eagerly approached and unlocked her collar. The chain dropped limply to the concrete, and she stood for a moment, massaging her neck where the cold iron had been clasped tightly over her tender skin.

Hubert didn't know what to do. She glanced over her shoulder, then moved off into the darkness. "Show me how to get the hell out of here!" she said as she weaved through the rubble.

More than willing to please her, Hubert raced ahead happily. "This way! I'm Hubert. Vesuvius always called me that. Do you have a name?"

"Just get us out of here," she snapped while climbing over chunks of brick and rusted metal.

She looked up once at the multitude of stars above them. Hubert seemed to be going too slowly for her, because she paused on more than one occasion and shot him a cold, impatient look.

"I was born here," Hubert felt compelled to say. "I learned how to speak so the Naga could tell me what to do. Are there a lot of people where you come from?"

Under her breath, she replied, "The Naga have already killed most of them."

She didn't look at Hubert again, but continued to search the stars while following him through the silent city. Hubert couldn't help but glance over his shoulder repeatedly. Vesuvius was both formidable and resourceful, and if they couldn't get out of the city quickly enough, they weren't going to get out at all.

They raced over broken roads without pausing for breath. She didn't seem at all interested in anything that Hubert tried to coax out of her. She was a trained survivor, well-practiced at fleeing the Naga hunting parties. Hubert couldn't help but embrace the strange thrill that made his heart race. Vesuvius would surely maim him if he was caught, and the girl would likely end up suffering a far worse fate.

She wasn't going to replace him.

He had to believe it wasn't too late to turn back, but whenever he stared at her long, lustrous tangle of black hair flowing over her shoulders, he felt as if he was being pulled after her. She was tireless, and soon wore him out. The point of no return seemed to break over the sky in the form of an approaching dawn, a faint blue light overtaking the darkness. They finally fled the city and found themselves in the wasted desert, and Hubert glanced over his shoulder a final time, and believed that he wouldn't regret leaving the only home he'd ever known.

They finally stopped near a gathering of old, rusted heaps of scrap metal that were once cars. She rested her back against a car door and sat near a pile of broken glass. Hubert sat down beside her, his legs twisted beneath him on the cool ground.

"You can never be forgiven for what you've done," she said.

"Vesuvius can't hurt me anymore," was all he could think to say while staring pathetically at a burn mark on his forearm, something he'd once earned from his old master.

"I should tell you that there's an army coming this way, she said. "The Naga are nearly extinct. They aren't any kind of civilization. They're nothing more than a bunch of freaks and mutants. They're a disease, and they'll be wiped out."

Hubert nodded. "I think that's good. I think maybe I'll like being with humans."

"Oh no, you're not coming with me," she said.

Her horizontal movement across his face was a blur, and the sudden pain that flared along his neck prompted him to bring his hands to his throat. Sticky, warm blood gushed out over his hands, and he fell back, gasping for air. What had she done to him? He'd saved her life!

"But I'm just like you. I'm one of you," Hubert struggled to say.

"No." She stood over him, a long piece of bloody glass in her hand. "You're nothing like me."

He tried to call out for Vesuvius but only frothy bubbles of blood came forth.

HOPELESSLY DEVOTED

KELLY M. HUDSON

Bullets were useless.

Any numbskull who'd lived this long would know that. And yet, some idiot was out there, popping off rounds like a drunk shooting fireworks at a Fourth of July picnic. That sound was sure to bring them running, if anything would, and whoever was stupid enough to be doing it was going to just as surely be dead in a few moments.

I listened, waited, and listened some more. The gunfire continued, sporadic now, a spray and burst here and there. Then it quieted, and I heard them, snarling, sifting through what was left of the street below, headed right towards the noise.

Babies.

That's what I called them. Babies. Mostly because that's what they reminded me of. They were small and flesh-colored, with flat bony plates covering their arms and legs. They crawled on all fours and if you just saw them from the face forward, you'd think they were babies. I think that's how so many got killed early on; people were just confused. You see an infant crawling around all alone, and you go out and try to pick it up and help it. These Babies had teeth, though: long, pointed, hidden by fat purple lips. They varied in sizes but none were bigger than three feet long and about two feet tall from palms to back.

They had that plating, like I said, which was nothing more than solid bone, which protected their upper half, the side pointing to the sky. Nothing I'd seen could get through that covering short of a rocket. I'd seen men fire the biggest guns you've ever heard of and the bullets would ping off, leaving behind at most a scorch mark. Armor piercing bullets did a little better. Sometimes they'd crack the shell, but I'd never seen one go all the way through. And the Babies would roll up into balls when they got fired on. They'd roll up and wait for a break in the action, unfold, scamper as fast as their little stump legs could carry them, and roll up again when the next rounds came.

Babies ran fast, too. They covered twenty yards in five seconds, no problem, at their slowest. So they were quick, and hard to shoot, and that wasn't all.

Beneath the pink plates were their bodies, and they were fleshy, almost doughy, with four long legs that ended in spiked claws. Those claws were good for just about anything. They could dig faster than a dog and tear through steel like it was wood. They were especially good at carving up skin and bone. The Babies would hook their victims with their claws and drag them off to their lairs underground, when they weren't just tearing them apart to eat on the spot.

That's where they came from: beneath our feet. And that's where they went back.

Some other things about them: they didn't come out as much during the day, but you were never safe in the sunlight. Nights were the worst. They'd scour any area in seconds because there were thousands of them. And people weren't the only things they ate. They liked animals, too, and plants. They were omnivores, but their favorite food was easily human beings.

I peered around over the edge of the rubble strewn about the floor of the building I was hiding in. There were six of them, scuttling over the wreckage of a burnt-out car, headed in the direction of the sounds of the shots. The sun was setting in the distance, throwing a glowing orange glow over the horizon, making the overhanging dust clouds bleed red. Pretty soon it would be night, and that half-dozen out there would turn into forty or fifty or more.

A few more shots rang out, echoing through the buildings. I shook my head. What an idiot. It was probably someone who'd lost their mind and was a gibbering fool. There were plenty of those left in the world. They usually didn't last long. I knew one guy who'd been perfectly normal one day, woke up the next, and shed his clothes. He laughed and glared at me, drool dripping from the corner of his mouth.

"I'm going dancing," he said, and he skipped out of the room that me and the group I was with at the time were hiding in, and down the stairs. He sang some old religious hymn at the top of his lungs.

He made it to the stoop outside before the Babies got him.

Later that night, they came for us. That was the last group I shacked up with. From then on out, I was purely solo.

Lightning flashed in the distance, inside the dust clouds. Electric rain, I called it, and it was coming my way. It always traveled in those kinds of clouds and when they poured, they shocked the hell out of you.

It was like having thousands of wet drops of snapping static electricity pop all around. There was no safe place from electric rain, except for a plain concrete room—which was pretty much where I was at the moment—or a dense forest. The wood and leaves absorbed the shocks in a way few other things did.

The only good thing about electric rain is it kept the Babies at bay. They didn't like it. Many were the nights it would pour and I'd hear them out there, howling in pain. Those were the nights I should have been sleeping, getting as much rest as I could, but I wouldn't.

Instead, I would sit up and listen to them cry out, and I'd think of my wife and son, long-since dead now. And I'd smile, hoping some of those lousy sonsabitches were dying out there.

I was in a city somewhere. I couldn't tell you where. There used to be signs. There used to be ways of finding out where you were, even if it was something left over, like a map or a street sign or a building placard. But almost all of that stuff was gone now, either burnt off in the rain or scavenged by survivors.

The truth is, most of the cities were completely gone by that point. They were wiped out in the tactical nuclear strikes some brilliant General must have thought would wipe out the Babies.

Those brilliant Generals were wrong, though, about that and everything else. The Babies were an enemy that came from below, and there was no end to them. It was like stamping out an anthill using a needle as your weapon. You were never going to win.

The Babies weren't the cause of the condition the world was in right now, but they didn't help out much. Things were going south well before they erupted from the ground and introduced themselves. We were already on our way to falling apart; the Babies were just the final straw.

Everything had kind of gone haywire at once. Weather turned weird, like the poles had flipped or something. People got strange, too, and mean. There was a rash of murders and disappearances. This was followed by a round of mass suicides. Nobody knew what was going on but everyone was freaking out. I can remember those days, sitting at home with my wife, watching the news, shaking my head, worrying.

Whatever was infecting the world, whatever madness was possessing folks, it hadn't come to our small Kentucky town yet. Not yet. So we couldn't really understand it and never did try to explain it. In the end, it didn't matter where it came from or why. Maybe God was done with humans as a species. Maybe it was some viral infection. Maybe the world was too cramped and people were having some kind of mass claustrophobia. I don't know. I'll never know. I just know how it all went down, when things got dark out there. I remember wars being declared and country turning against country. I remember Canada becoming incensed and sending troops down into Detroit.

I remember Mexico invading Texas, claiming it was theirs by right. And I remember our Second Civil War, right in the midst of all the other shit going down. The South split from the rest of the country, declared the Confederacy alive and well, and the planes and tanks came in from Ohio and the surrounding states. This time, Kentucky wasn't neutral, and pretty soon, we had militias and blackouts and food rationing and all kinds of insanity. Through it all, me and my wife and our three-year-old-son kept to ourselves, praying for the best and expecting the worst.

And there, right then, when things got on the verge of completely falling apart, the Babies came. What they were, nobody knew. Where they came from was easy enough: up out of the ground.

Some scientists, in the early days, suspected they were from deep within the earth, beyond range of most of their underground radars. Some thought they were dinosaurs from ancient times, hibernating. Hippies said they were sleeping down there and had been woken up by oil drilling. Preachers said they were demons. Conservatives blamed the liberals and liberals blamed the conservatives. In any case, they wiped out most of us within a week.

We lost so much so fast because their spread was rapid and decisive. Add to it the fact that we were all spread out, fighting amongst each other and distracted by all our prejudices and hates. The Babies took out humanity pretty easily.

In the last days, before my wife and son died, before the TVs turned off for good and the radio went the way of electricity, we saw the Babies weren't just appearing in America, but the rest of the world, too. We saw the reports and the footage from Russia, Africa, Australia...everywhere. It didn't seem like anywhere was immune.

Pretty soon, all that were left were pockets of survivors, hiding out, fighting for scraps of food, for shelter, for protection. I learned pretty quick it was signing up for suicide to stick with those groups, and I headed out on my own.

Now I was here, in the remains of some city, high off the ground where it was safest, listening to some fool rile up a small gang of Babies.

I kept watch outside, figuring I could at least keep track of the little bastards and where they were. When night came, like I said before, more of them would appear. They would scour the area, searching for any scrap of food. When they didn't find any, I would watch them sometimes turn against each other. Those were some epic battles. I remember one night—was it a month ago or a year? I couldn't keep track anymore—when I saw about three dozen of them in a big courtyard, going at it. They didn't stop until there was something like ten left. Those ten ate like kings.

It was smart to see where they came from because, odds were, the others would appear from the same spot. They weren't particularly smart when it came to hiding or covering their tracks, but then again, they didn't have to be. Their main enemies, humanity, were practically wiped out.

In this case, they came from a hole on the other side of the building I was hiding in. It was down near a burnt-out window on the southern end and was as wide as a car.

They scrambled out and headed towards the noise, moving fast and even, keeping an equal distance between each other, spreading out but staying close. That was how they hunted. They learned pretty quick in the early days that some humans had grenades and dynamite, so they had to make sure they didn't get bunched up or they could get killed in large groups.

The sounds were coming from down the street. The road itself had big holes punched in it, some dripping down into a sewer system beneath and others full of dirt. The blacktop was smashed into bits, like a giant had decided to stomp around for a while. A few wrecked cars, their parts stripped and left like discarded insect shells to rust in the sun and melt in the electric rain. There was rubble, and at the end, where the road curved out of my line of sight, was a big heap of what looked like the remains of a small building. That was where the shots were coming from, and that was where the Babies were headed.

I kept an eye on them until they reached the building and then ducked back inside where I was. There would be nothing left to see. From here on, it would be screams followed by silence. If I were lucky, I wouldn't hear their claws click together as they carved whomever the stupid person was shooting off their gun.

The room I was in was barren, which was no surprise. Like I said before, looters and survivors had long ago ripped through what was left of the cities. I was staring at an empty room, with a stone floor that used to be covered in some kind of white linoleum, not much of which was left. There were a few scraps in the corner, where whoever had stripped it up had either gotten in a hurry or decided they'd had enough. What someone needed with linoleum, I couldn't say, but I'd seen stranger mysteries out in the world.

At the end of the room was a doorway into the hall, which led to the stairs. I had climbed up here yesterday to get some rest and found it to be a good spot. I hadn't seen any Babies until today and there was enough of a roof overhead to keep the rain from finding me. The entire eastern wall was missing, though, except for a hunk in the corner where I was currently ducked down, taking the occasional look-see outside.

I thought I found a really good place to hole up in, but I was wrong. I was practically sitting on a nest of Babies, and even if I thought that fool out there with the gun was an idiot, I suppose I should have thanked him for bringing them running. Now I at least knew the danger I was in.

More gunshots rang out, followed by the screams. It wouldn't be long now. The gunfire became more rapid, following fast one after another. The screams stopped. The bullets did not. Then I heard something else, a sound I thought had long gone extinct in this world.

I heard a woman shouting.

I peered around the corner, and sure enough, here ran a skinny little thing, gun in hand, Babies hot on her heels. She was maybe five and a half feet tall and made of toothpicks. I swear, when you used to see those stick figure drawings kids made, she could have been the living embodiment of one. She was almost naked, with tatters of a shirt and jeans clinging to her fragile form, and a backpack riding on her shoulders. She had only clumps of hair to speak of, and that spoke of either mange or radiation poisoning. Could be both.

Here's the thing: as surprised as I was to see a woman, and just as surprised she was still alive this long, I was also pissed at her. And that was because she was running right towards the building I was hiding in and effectively bringing the Babies right to me.

Stupid, stupid, stupid.

She spun and fired twice, the bullets biting the dirt in front of a couple of them. Those two rolled into balls and skidded to a halt. The other four kept right on coming. They didn't seem to be in a big hurry, either. They knew they were faster than her, just like they knew she wasn't going to get away. It was only a matter of when they decided to eat her, not '*if.*'

The girl screeched and ran faster, putting a little distance between them and her. The two who'd rolled up now unfolded and watched. They turned and ran back the way they'd come, apparently chasing after other game.

The four bastards still chasing her were making a game of it. Two of them split off and ran to her right and two to her left, hemming her in. They were steering her towards the hole they'd come out of and, thus, to my building.

She was too busy running to notice. What she did see, though, was me. She glanced up, spotted me peeking, and yelled.

"Help me!"

I ducked back around.

"Hell," I said, to no one in particular. "Hell."

I didn't have much time and it didn't pay to sit around and feel sorry for myself. Like everything at that point in my miserable existence, I tried to reduce my worries to the most immediate concerns. First, I had to get ready for the Babies. Second, I had to deal with them. Third, I had to run.

First things first.

I jumped up and sprinted out of the room and to the stairs. There was a wall that served as a railing along the side, which I could duck down and hide behind. I did that. I crouched and edged towards the end, and waited.

I pulled my long knife. Unfortunately, in dealing with Babies, the best way, the only way, was to kill them up close. And that meant you put yourself in a hell of a lot of danger. It was why I stayed away, trying to remain hidden and unnoticed, rather than going out, guns blazing. There was no way I could be discreet now, though, since the lady had blown my cover, so I had to deal with them.

She clomped across the floor downstairs and I don't mind admitting that, in the moment, I hoped they would catch her and take her down before she could get any closer. It wasn't out of meanness, but out of survival. My life would be a lot easier if they got her.

Her frantic footsteps up the stairs meant I was going to have to deal with things the hard way.

"Hell," I said, under my breath. I slid out the duct tape I carried in my backpack, tore a long piece off with my teeth, and wrapped it around the knife in my hand. There was no way I could drop it now and, if they were going to get me, they were also going to get six inches of pure, gleaming steel.

I stayed in my crouch and waited.

She was close to the top now and then there she was, dashing past me, not even seeing me.

The first Baby popped around the corner. With my free hand, I grabbed the back of its bony armor, flipped it, and plunged my blade into its stomach. It screeched. Red blood sputtered from the wound and splattered the floor and the wall by the stairs. Its legs and arms kicked and clawed at me but I had already dropped it on its back and shoved it away like a hockey puck. It skittered into the corner, a long streak of blood in its wake.

The second one was around the corner before it saw what had happened to its brother. I did the same to it, flipping, stabbing, and throwing. It howled, too, and clattered against its dying mate in the corner.

The third took a long loop around the corner, but I had been expecting that. I leapt out, diving for it, the knife slashing at its head. I missed. The blade caught the floor, throwing up chunks of concrete and sparks. The Baby screamed and veered to its left, down the hallway. I wouldn't get another shot at it.

But the fourth one was already on me, hissing and pinching my right calf. I wore chain mail I found in another town in the remains of some Renaissance Fair that had been ravaged by the creatures. It was the real deal and came in two pieces: one for the torso, the other for the legs. More than once it'd saved my life and it did so again. That's not to say the little bastard didn't hurt me. The mail may have kept it from ripping my leg off, but it did slash and bruise the skin beneath. It also tripped me up. I landed on my stomach.

I grunted, rolled over, and kicked its face. There's nothing more insulting to one of those things than a nice boot to the head. It squalled and cantered, it claws digging the floor and snapping at me like some kind of swollen lobster.

I was on all fours now, scrambling around like a dog, facing the creature. It smiled, its human-like, tiny face eerily like an angry child's.

They always got cocky like this. They thought they were invincible, and when you met them down on the ground, face-to-face, they felt they had the upper hand. This made them stupid. So when it charged at me, I stifled a giggle as I drove the knife up under its chin and stabbed it through the head.

Baby Number Four collapsed to the side, twitching.

I yanked the knife out and waited for the other two. I would have waited a long time if the girl they'd been chasing hadn't come up behind me and spoken.

"They didn't come after me," she said. Her voice was clear and pretty, like a bell ringing. It jarred me. How long had it been since I'd heard another person's voice? I couldn't remember.

"They went after the rapists," she said. Which made no sense to me, but whatever. If she was right, and they were gone, it was time for me to do the same.

I stood and she stepped to me. I tried not to look at her but it was hard not to. She blinked up at me. She was so tiny, and her eyes were so blue. I looked away. Getting close to somebody would get you killed.

"Thanks for saving me," she said.

I pushed her aside. I almost stopped and apologized when she yelped and tumbled to the floor. But I kept going. Sentiment was nice in the old world. Here, it got you the business end of the claws of the Babies.

Plus, there was that other Baby, hidden somewhere up here, waiting to get us.

I jogged into the room. My pack was lying on the floor, and next to it, my sleeping bag. I stupidly had not rolled it up this morning, something I did every day. You always have to be ready to move and being unpacked was just plain dumb.

I briefly considered ditching it but that was worse than leaving it out. That bag was waterproof and warm as hell. There was no way I was getting rid of it.

I rolled it up, attached it to the pack, slung the whole deal on my back, and tromped back towards the stairs.

The girl stood in my way, arms folded, bottom lip thrust out. This time, I got a good look at her.

She was short and skinny, all angles except for her hips, which curved like a bend in the earth, nice and easy. But her knees and elbows were jagged, and her arms and legs were about the width of an old half-dollar coin. She was flat chested and had no ass. Her face was pretty, though. It reminded me of an elf in one of those Hobbit movies. Her eyes were blue, like diamonds, and her hair, what was left of it, was platinum blonde.

"Well, that was rude," she said, her voice exasperated.

I pushed past her again. I didn't knock her down this time. I bounded down the stairs, knife still taped to my hand. I was ready. If the other Baby came, I was ready. It never did, though. It had disappeared and I never saw it again.

My next move was to get far away. That required running, which I was good at, and going in the right direction, which was always a guessing game. When I exited the building, I chose east, away from the hole in the ground. There were more buildings out there and, just beyond them, a forest. In the distance, the sky rumbled with black clouds heading my way. Flashes of lightning lit them up, making them sparkle like big puffs of chocolate ice cream with candy sprinkles.

I glanced left and right. In the distance, back where the girl had been shooting her gun, a couple of screams echoed, drifting between the ruins and over the burnt-out cars. So, she hadn't been lying. Someone else had been out there, and the other Babies had really gone after them. Good. That bought me some time.

The Babies would come out of their hole, smell the spilt blood of their brothers, and investigate. Then they would come looking for me. The first place they'd go would be the buildings. The forest was too far away, especially with the rains coming, and there was a big, open field lying before the forest. No shelter if the rain caught them. Of course, it meant no shelter for me, either, but I had some time, and I was going to use it.

I sprinted, my boots digging into the shards of concrete and tufts of dirt beneath my feet. I could move pretty fast when I wanted to, but my best advantage was my endurance. I could run or walk for a long, long time. Time wasn't on my side here; speed was my deliverance, if I didn't want to get stuck in that field with a bunch of crackling and popping rain burning my skin.

The clouds rolled closer and I dashed towards them. It was like we were destined to meet, head to head, man against nature. I would lose, no doubt about it, if things came down to that. But if I could make the treeline and get under the leaves, I should be fine. The wood would act as a natural stopper to the sparking rain and I was pretty sure I could handle the few drops that made it through. I'd been in worse spots before.

Those clouds were getting darker by the moment, roiling and boiling, churning the space between them and me. Bright blue sparks of lightning shot through them, slashing the sky. A few struck the ground, here and there, but never too close to me. Not close enough to make me worry, that is. I wasn't sure I could make it, but I was too far gone now to stop. I'd reached the field and the closest building was about the same distance away as the trees.

It's amazing what you can get used to, and how your body can adapt, when it comes down to survival. In my old life, I was an accountant. I sat at a desk, ran an adding machine, and filled in ledgers. Before that, I was an okay athlete in college, but never better than the intramural teams I played on. I got fat from all the sitting at my job. Not sit on a chair and break it fat, but fairly chubby. My wife used to tease me relentlessly, but that's the kind of relationship we had. It was good, and whenever I thought of her and my son, I got sad enough to eat a bullet. So I tried to never think of them.

Now, after a year of this kind of life, I was more fit than I'd ever been. And proud of it. But that's how it is, when you're constantly on the run, always looking over your shoulder. You get good or you get dead, and when it came to running, I was the best.

I reached the trees just as the clouds broke and the rain gushed down like Niagara Falls. I stopped, leaned against a big oak next to me, and took a moment to catch my breath.

Standing next to me was that damned woman. And she wasn't even breathing hard.

"I get it if you don't want me around, but you don't have to be a dick about it," she said. She wasn't pouting anymore. She was mad. Her arms were crossed, her head was cocked to one side, and her hips were jutting in the opposite direction as her head.

I turned and walked away. Would this never end? She was like a puppy, and I wondered if at some point I'd have to kick her to keep her away.

I plunged deeper into the woods. It got dark in there. With the clouds above blotting out what was left of the afternoon, and the natural, thick shade of the leaves, most of the light was gone. It wasn't quite night in there, but it was getting close.

My eyes were good in the dark. It was another habit I'd learned in my time of survival. You have to be able to see well at night. I wasn't like an owl, but I was pretty darned good.

"You better duck," she said from behind me.

I ignored her. There wasn't…

I bonked my head on a low-lying branch I didn't see. It hurt like hell. She giggled. That hurt even worse.

I ducked, too late, and kept going. The air turned chilly and I shivered. I wanted to get my small jacket from inside my pack and put it on.

I had gotten used to the cold by now—another of my survival adaptations—but it was getting pretty darned frigid out, and wearing an extra coat wouldn't hurt.

The girl walked ahead of me, slipping out of her jacket.

"I'm burning up," she said.

Damn her.

I didn't pull out my coat. I didn't slow down. In fact, I sped up so I was ahead of her again. She might have bested me in a lot of things, but by God, I was going to out-walk her.

"Quit following me," she said, snarling over her shoulder. She was moving too quickly for me to pass. I could keep pace, but she was like a jaguar, sliding over fallen trees, gliding across the grass.

I decided that was a good idea, so I turned to my right and broke into a sprint. I was pretty sure I'd lost her when I came around a big elm tree and there she was, striding just ahead of me.

Damn her.

She looked back and sighed.

"Well, I guess you can stick with me, if you want."

It went on like that for a good while, until I felt like I'd put enough distance between us and the Babies. Between me and the Babies.

I discovered a clearing just ahead, where the trees reached over, their limbs and leaves intertwining, creating a canopy. There was only soft grass in the small area; no rocks or downed trees.

I stopped, took off my pack, and stretched. All I had to do was check out the surrounding area, make sure there were no Baby holes lying in wait, and then I felt like I could build a very small fire and maybe get some sleep.

She was there, of course, sitting Indian-style in the middle of the clearing. She glanced up when I arrived and frowned.

"I guess we can share this area," she said. "But just remember: I got here first."

"Shut up," I said, letting my pack hit the ground.

"Oh! He speaks! And it's not in grunts, either. Maybe there's hope for you."

I glared at her, looked at my pack, and reconsidered leaving it there while I took a quick look around. What if she took off with it?

"I'm not going to bother your stuff," she said. She pulled an apple out of her pocket and chomped into it. An apple? When was the last time I'd seen one of those? Man, I couldn't remember.

"I'm not a thief," she said. "And besides, you smell. I can't imagine your clothes would be any better."

"If you don't like my smell, then why don't you leave?"

"Nope. I got here first. Why don't you leave?"

That was a good question. I left my bag alone and walked the perimeter, checking it out. Nothing could sneak up on us in the middle there, as long as we kept watch, so that was good. And there were plenty of options as far as getting away. We could run in any direction and it was pretty clear sailing no matter which way we went.

"We're fine," she said. She took another bite from the apple. It was a small one, and green, so I imagined it was pretty tart. I had a neighbor when I was a kid who had an apple tree that rained apples like that. He always said if you ate too many of the green kind, you'd get the runs. I never ate enough to find out, but I suspected he was right.

"How do you know?" I said.

She tapped the side of her head. "I got smarts," she said.

The smell of that apple was filling the area. My stomach turned. I was pretty damned hungry. I wondered if she had another one hidden somewhere. I wasn't going to ask. She could take her fancy apples and shove them.

"I'll check anyway, if that's okay with you," I said.

"Suit yourself. I'm just going to sit here and eat my apple."

Damn her.

I built a fire. She sure didn't mind sitting next to it.

"You're not going to give me a hard time?" I said.

"Hell, no. You built a fire. It was very manly of you."

She was grinning, but I wasn't.

"My name is Sandy, by the way," she said, eyes sparkling. She held her hand out for me to shake. I looked away.

"I don't want to know your name," I said.

"Why not? That's stupid."

"No, it's not. Knowing your name is the first step to growing attached. You grow attached, it hurts more when those things out there eat you. And they will eat you."

"Stupid," she said. She was quiet for a while and I thought I might actually get some peace, but I was foolish.

"My mom named me Sandy after that girl in that movie, Grease. Have you seen it?"

I shook my head.

"Liar," she said. "Every boy's seen it, if they've ever had a girl-friend. Because that's what good girlfriend's do: they make their boys watch heart-warming movies."

She was right. I had seen it. Many, many times. It was my wife's favorite film. Mine was *The Five Heartbeats*, if that counts for anything. We both liked musicals, I guess.

I kept my mouth shut. She didn't.

"Then again, you're the kind of guy I could see not ever having a girlfriend because you're really ugly and, yeah, you stink," she said, wrinkling her nose. "I know things are kind of tight out here, but there are rivers and streams. You could take a bath."

"Why would I?"

"In case a pretty girl comes along."

"I tell you what: you let me know when one shows up, and I'll be sure to run off and scrub myself clean."

"As long as you promise to wash behind your ears."

There was no getting to her. I'd never met anyone so...happy...in my life. Ever. Not even before the world went to hell. Nobody like her. It infuriated me.

"So my mom loved that movie and I watched it all the time. I learned all the songs, front and back, even the boy's parts," she said.

I stared at the fire.

"I could sing some for you, if you want."

"Are you crazy?"

"Sure. Isn't everybody?"

"My God. Will you ever shut up?"

"Nope. Can't do that. I like to keep the art of conversation in practice. I talk to myself all the time, as well as sing. And when I run into somebody, I take the opportunity to speak with them and listen, too."

"Did you try and talk to the rapists?"

At this, her cheery disposition took a turn. I swear I saw a dark cloud form on her forehead.

"No," she hissed. "They're not much for talking."

Rapists. They were all over the place. Of the survivors of this current mess we found ourselves in, more men had made it than women. When things started to get even worse, I saw plenty of men in the groups I was with turn on the women, taking what they wanted. Some fought back, others gave up.

It was really a return to the caveman days, and one of the reasons I split from everyone. I couldn't abide by their actions, and most times, there was no way to stop them. They worked in packs, and would take turns, so when one was getting his jollies, the others would keep watch. And by 'keep watch,' I mean stand around and eyeball the goings on as well as whoever else was around, just to make sure they didn't try anything.

I was always outnumbered, so I walked away. I went from group to group, and as sure as there was a sun in the sky, if there was a woman in the group, at some point it would turn to raping, if it hadn't already.

I hate people. "Sorry," I said.

She waved me away. She was sitting on the ground, holding her hands out by the fire, enjoying its warmth.

"Thanks for building the fire. I haven't been warm in forever."

"No problem," I said. "It may not be smart, but I think we're far enough away from anybody or anything else. We should be okay."

"Well, if not, it was worth it. 'Live every moment like it's your last,' my mom used to say. I never got it back then, but I sure do get it now."

Another look came over her, more wistful and sad. Seeing it made me sad, too. It made me think of my wife and my son and what happened to them the night the Babies attacked our house. I tried to never think of that night, but sometimes, you know, you can't help yourself. I shook off the memories.

She did the same, it seemed, as the smile returned to her face. And I have to say, she had a nice smile. She was rail-thin, and held next to no allure for me, both physically and personality-wise. But she did have a nice smile.

"I'll take first watch," she said. "If you want to sleep."

I woke up four hours later in the pitch black of the night. The fire had died to embers. Sandy was supposed to wake me but hadn't. Instead, she was behind me, pressed in against my back, curled like a little kitten, sharing her body warmth.

At first, I got pissed. And then I got tired. So I went back to sleep. Damn her.

The next morning I resolved to make her go her own way. Of course, telling Sandy what to do was like telling the wind which direction to blow. They were going to do what they wanted.

She was up before me, ready to go. She was also eating another apple, and since I hadn't eaten for nearly a day now, my mouth started watering like crazy when I smelled it.

"You want one?" she said. I really wanted to say yes, but my pride kept my lips sealed. Stupid, stupid pride.

"Suit yourself," she said, shrugging. She turned and faced off towards the west. "I think if we head that way, we'll go deeper into the woods. I think that will put us really far from the little creeps and the rapists, which is smart thinking, if you ask me."

She was right. The Babies tended to avoid the forests for some reason I couldn't fathom, and if there were any rapists about, they would surely not give a damn about going out into the woods. They preferred buildings and shelter to sleeping out in the wild.

"Okay," I said, and let her lead the way.

We walked for half an hour before she started up again.

"So, seriously, what's your name? You can tell me. It's okay."

"No," I said. "I didn't even want to know yours."

"Too late," she said, her voice a singsong of sassafras. "Elvis has left the building."

"What does that mean?"

She whirled, a giggle on her lips. "Is that it? You're named Elvis, aren't you? Oh, it has to be that!"

"My name is not Elvis."

"Maybe not, but it's something embarrassing, or else you'd tell me. I'm right, aren't I?"

"Leave me alone."

"I knew it!" she jogged over and slugged my shoulder. How did she have such energy? Maybe it was the apples.

"I've got an idea," I said, remembering back to the old days. "We can play a game."

"Ooo! I like that!" she said, her blue eyes sparkling. Did I mention she had pretty eyes? Well, she did. That and a nice smile. The rest of her, though, good God. Skinny-minny. "Is the game called *Guess My Name*?"

"No," I said. "It's called The Game of Silence. Whoever talks first loses."

"Lame," she said. "Boring. Weak."

"Okay, I got it."

"Ooo!" she said. She was dancing around me like a little kid with a big decision to make between Disneyland or Disneyworld.

"I like my idea better. Guess your name." She placed a finger to her lips, thinking. "It has to be something embarrassing, so what could it be...?"

"I like The Game of Silence better."

"You would. And that's because you have a weird name, don't you...Norman?"

"No."

"Billy-Bob."

"No."

"You sure? You do seem like a hillbilly."

"No."

"Maybe it's a girl's name. I had an uncle named Laverne once. Is that your name? Are you a Laverne?"

"Only if you're named Shirley."

She scrunched up her face. "I don't get it."

"You're too young to."

"What about Sammi, with an 'I' ?"

"No."

"Then it must be something like Fred. Nobody would want to be named Fred, not even a big Scooby-Doo fan."

I shook my head and kept walking.

"Oh!" she laughed. "That is it! I got you!"

"No. It's not."

"Yes, it is! And even if it isn't, that's what it's gonna be, since you won't tell me."

She stopped in front of me and held her hand out for me to shake.

"Nice to meet you, Fred. As in Flintstone. As in 'yabba-dabba-doo.' I'm Sandy, as in, 'tell me more tell me more.' "

I batted her hand to the side. Softly, though.

As I walked on, she laughed. "Don't be like that. Fred."

Damn her.

We stumbled upon a small pack of Babies later that afternoon.

It was a total accident, and I think they were just as surprised as we were. I trailed behind Sandy; there was just no way of catching completely up with her. She walked almost as fast as she talked, and, like her mouth, her legs never got tired.

We took a couple of breaks, but I think mostly it was because she saw me panting and trying to play tough. I was glad she did, because my feet were about to fall off.

Two breaks, fifteen minutes the first one and thirty the second, and we were on our way again.

Part of the reason she was pushing so hard was because the forest had thinned out and the blanket of leaves above us parted, revealing a sky that alternated between black and purple, like a bruise mixing just below the skin.

It could pour electric rain at any moment, and you could feel it, hanging in the air, just waiting to happen. Like a pause in a great song. When the hairs on your neck and arms stand up, you know you're close to getting the ever-loving God shocked out of you.

It was this hurry, and her flapping lips, that caused us to stagger unawares into a big meadow blooming with crab grass and daisies. And Babies. Four of them.

The closest, a big mother, about twice the size of a bulldog, was so surprised I swear it must have jumped about ten feet into the air. When it landed, though, it spun, and snarled, as did the other three directly behind it.

For the life of me, I will never know just what those Babies were up to out there, but I knew what they were going to be up to now: attacking, killing, and feasting.

Sandy and I froze, both jarred. We were damned lucky they were just as shocked, or they would have killed us easy.

The first one, the big one, leapt towards Sandy, scuttling across the field, covering the ten yards between her and it in seconds. She didn't have time to react. Fortunately, I was right behind her because I'd finally caught up. Also fortunately, I had one of my many knives handy. As it leapt up off the ground, its claws clicking and its jaws snapping, I dove under it.

I shoved the knife up, carving its tender underbelly. A gob of red blood spurted out, followed by a long trail of intestines.

Somehow, the creature's innards had gotten stuck to the end of my knife, so as it sailed over me, I pulled its guts out. The Baby hit the ground, rolled, howled, and turned to charge me. It was so angry, it didn't know it was already dead.

The three behind me wasted no time and, in those split seconds, I was pinned between the two factions. Sandy, though, had recovered.

The nearest Baby of the three leapt.

I rolled over, yanking my knife free of the intestines from the bigger one, and braced myself for the impact.

An apple struck its forehead, stunning it. The Baby looked up and veered to the right and I swear I saw a halo of stars and exclamation points orbit its head as it stumbled and collapsed.

The other two, still coming on, were smart enough to toss themselves to the ground and roll up. The next apple that flew struck one on its shell and exploded into a thousand pieces.

I turned back to Sandy and stared. She had a hell of an arm on her.

"Look out!" she shouted.

The big one was almost on me. I laughed and kicked it with my boot. It staggered to the side, its mouth working open and shut, blood pulsing from between its lips. It just didn't want to give up, even though its guts were strewn about like lines of thick snot. It wobbled, cast a baleful gaze my way, farted, and died.

The other one, the Baby hit by the apple, got its senses back and churned dirt, heading my way.

I crouched and waited until it was almost on top of me. At the last second, I dove over it, grabbing the top of its shell. I flipped the Baby onto its back, slamming it to the earth. I followed with my knife, jabbing it in deep and twisting.

I jerked my hands back as its claws tried to clamp on my arm, missing by inches. When its legs and arms retracted, I plunged the knife back in, rapidly, chunking away as its hot blood spewed out. The Baby squalled and squirmed, but it was dead just a moment later.

That left the other two, which rolled up into balls.

I climbed to my feet and glared at them. They would unroll a tiny bit, their eyes peeking out, and duck back in when they saw me looking.

"What do we do?" Sandy asked.

I didn't say anything. I ran towards the closest, reared back with my leg, and kicked it with the flat of my foot. The Baby rolled over and opened, surprised at my attack. I jumped towards it, knife flashing. It hopped back, howling. I didn't like that. It could be calling others of its kind and, if it was, we were well and truly screwed.

The most ungodly scream erupted right behind me. It filled my ears and tickled my brain. I was about to turn around to see what it was when flashing past me came Sandy, running straight at the Baby wailing across from me.

She was waving her hands and pistoning her legs and, I have to say, scaring the hell out of me.

Whatever she was doing, it scared the Baby, too. It turned tail and ran. Its friend unrolled and ran, too. They were headed towards the end of the meadow, forty yards away, where a stand of trees stood. Beyond that was darkness.

The sky broke and the rain fell.

Big, plump drops struck the Babies, sparking on their shells. They shrieked and rolled into balls for protection as the electric water poured over them. They kept wiggling and screeching, the moisture getting into the cracks and stinging them mercilessly.

I wasted no more time. I ran at them, dropped to my knees, and jammed my knife in where I thought their soft parts were. I wriggled the blade until their blood was spurting out, butchering both of them.

Behind me, Sandy barked and ran for the trees. The electric rain hurt like hell, but we could stand it a lot longer than the Babies. I don't know the reason for that; I just know it's true.

My anger and determination, as well as my thick coat, kept me out in it a lot longer than I probably should have been. But I was pissed.

These things had a habit of popping up and killing a person, and I would be damned if they would get Sandy or me.

Plus, I still had to haul their corpses to the stand of trees so we could eat them later.

Baby meat is tough, but it's filling. I built a small fire—after making sure the rest of the area was clear of the little bastards—pried the meat from their shells, fashioned a couple of long sticks into kabobs, and roasted them over the open flame.

At first, Sandy turned up her nose. I was starting to think she was some kind of vegetarian, until the grease from the cooking meat ran off and sizzled in the fire. She licked her lips and, when I passed her a kabob, she nearly burned her tongue she gobbled it down so fast.

"This is good," she said.

"I figure it's only fair," I said. "They eat us. We might as well eat them."

So we ate, and it was good. We feasted until our bellies were round and hurting. We laughed a bit and she even sang one of the songs from *Grease*. But low, in case any other Babies were out there, lurking. When we finished, she started speaking again. As usual, I couldn't have stopped her if I wanted to, but in this case, she needed to say what she did. And I needed to hear it.

"I was part of a group of survivors out of Atlanta," she said. "There were ten of us, seven women, three men. We lived for a long time together. We found a nice spot over in Alabama that was pretty clear of the Babies and other people. We were pretty convinced we'd be okay, until the rapists came."

She shuddered and leaned in closer to the flames.

"It was in the middle of the night. I was fast asleep when they crept into our camp. They knifed the men first; all but Roy, who was the youngest. They hit him in the head with a rock. I wish it had killed him, because when he woke up, he was retarded. Or brain damaged. Or something. But by then it was too late for all of us. The rapists got to the women, too, beating some of us down until we couldn't move, or surprising the rest and holding us until we were hog-tied. Yeah, we were literally hog-tied."

She stuck out her hands, holding them over the flames. As she spoke, she lowered them, dropping closer and closer to the fire.

"They carried us back to their camp, which was a few miles away. As they did, they bragged a lot. 'We followed you for a long time,' one of them said. 'We're great trackers.' I tried not to listen, but when they started getting into details about what they were going to do to us, I couldn't shut it out. If they were trying to scare me, they were doing a good job. I hung there and was terrified. The next day, I found out they weren't exaggerating."

Her hands lowered. They were inches from the fire. She stared into the flames, never looking up. It was like she was gazing into the fires of hell and couldn't break the spell.

"Their camp held about twenty men, all of them about as ugly as a person could be. They were rangy, dirty and they stunk. They'd made a village out of spare wood, building small houses on top of sticks to keep them off the ground. The group that got us totaled five, so there were fifteen others that came out to greet us when we arrived the next dawn."

Her hands dipped. I thought I smelled burning flesh.

"They took Roy and drug him out in front of the group. He was babbling. Drool dripped from his mouth. His head was covered in dried blood and his eyes were crossed from the blow to his head. He'd also crapped his pants, but I couldn't really smell it over the stench of those other men. A big guy walked out, parting the others. 'Here comes Pauly,' one of them said. 'He don't like girls, but he sure does love a good manhole.' Pauly yanked his pants down and out popped the biggest dork I've ever seen. Four of the men pinned Roy to the ground and yanked his britches down. 'He done shit himself,' said one of them. 'That's okay,' Pauly said. 'I like it good and greased-up.' "

She paused. Tears rolled out of her eyes.

"That man split my friend Roy in two. He hammered him until Roy's eyes popped from his head, and he kept going a little longer after that."

Her hands lowered. The flames were practically licking the flesh.

"That got the rest of them good and worked-up. They swarmed us. Knives came out, ropes were cut, and my friends were rolled around. They were raped. All of them. Some on their stomachs, some on their backs, a few on their sides."

She paused again, swallowing hard.

"When they cut my rope, the bastard who was going to do me wasn't very bright, and he gave me a chance to slip free. I did. I ran. He took off after me. I kept going. I left my friends there to suffer and die. All I could think of was getting away, and that's what I did. I ran and ran. I can run pretty fast. I left that man behind, far behind. And pretty soon, it was evening, and I was completely lost, but I was free."

She snatched her hand away from the fire, wincing. Her eyes left the flames and bore in on me. Sandy stood, and she looked a lot like how I thought the Angel of Death must look.

She slipped out of her clothes as she walked over to me. By the time she stood before me, she was completely naked.

It was the most beautiful thing I'd ever seen.

"I tell you this because I want you to know: I'm not tainted. They didn't get to me. I'm whole and free," she said. "And I want you."

I grabbed her and pulled her to me. The rest of the night went by in a blur. Damn her.

*　*　*

In the morning, she rolled over and kissed my cheek.

"You still smell, but I like you anyway."

She bounced off and went behind a tree, squatting down. I sat up on one elbow and watched.

"Ew!" she yelled. "Don't watch me pee! That's gross!"

I laughed and turned away.

The rest of that morning we spent eating some of the leftover Baby meat and making love. It was a good morning. For the first time since this had all started, I felt real again, like a man. But more than that.

I felt like a human being. Life had a purpose again. In my mind, it became less about trying to survive to the next hour and more about, hey, let's find some place and hole up and just live. I wanted to hear her stories and I wanted to tell her mine.

I wanted to touch her, again and again, and hold her close. I wanted a new world, with bigger possibilities than running and hiding.

Because of her, I wanted a lot of things I never thought would be probable again. But with her, they felt as real and natural as a stream cutting through a forest.

It wasn't smart, though, to sit around that area too long. If some Babies had been there, it was a safe bet there'd be more at least reasonably close by. We packed up and headed out, going east.

The woods were thick and surprisingly untouched. I didn't know where the hell I was anymore and that was okay with me.

Sandy had said she was in Alabama when she ran, so I figured I was still somewhere in the South, and since I hadn't stumbled across a giant river, I must still be somewhere east of the Mississippi.

Not that it mattered.

We strolled, taking it easy. There weren't many animals around, but that was no shock. The Babies ate them, too, and the bigger mammals were long-gone by now. Deer and cows and dogs were the first to go.

I imagined there were still plenty of skunks and possums and squirrels because they were either too gross to kill and eat or too fast.

There were plenty of birds. We heard them chirping as we walked and I swear to God, it was almost like they were serenading us.

Like they were thrilled to see two actual, living human beings still tromping around. Then again, one did crap on my shoulder, so there's that.

"That's good luck!" Sandy cried when the white gunk splattered on my shoulder.

"What?"

"That's what my mom always used to say. A bird poops on you, it's good luck," she said. She turned, kissed my cheek, and smiled. "You're a lucky guy."

I sure was. I grabbed her and kissed her lips, dipping my shoulder so it rubbed the bird poo on her cheek.

"You bastard!" she laughed, squealing and running away from me. I ran after her.

When I caught up, she showed me just how lucky I really was.

We spent three blissful days together before the rapists found us.

There had been no more Baby sightings, the electric rain had stopped, the sun beamed its light and grace down upon us, and

Sandy eventually shared some of her apples. We made love. We danced. She sang to me. I sang to her.

We ate the rest of the Baby meat, drank from a cool, clear spring we followed for miles, and we slept under the stars.

It was paradise. It felt like we were Adam and Eve, let back into the Garden. It was the finest time of my life.

The first to arrive was a man I would come to know as Randy. He was tall and skinny and didn't look like much, but he was a wiry bastard, and stronger than he appeared.

He was shirtless and had one of those chests that curved inward, ribs that jutted out like claws, and a giant chin with clumps of bristling hairs as thin and sharp as porcupine quills.

He emerged from the woods, hunched over, running nearly on all fours. When I first saw him, I thought I was hallucinating, because it was early morning and I'd just woken up. Sandy was still asleep.

"My name is Randy," he shouted. "And I feel dandy."

I reached for a knife when something heavy and hard smashed the back of my head.

It was some time later when I woke, and it was to the sound of a man screaming.

I swam up out of my delirium to watch as another guy, whose name I never got, danced around in a circle, hands clutching his crotch, blood streaming from between his legs.

My hands were bound behind my back and my shoulders were on fire.

"That bitch!" he shrieked.

Sandy was on her knees, tied and held down by two other men, one of whom was Randy. She had blood on her mouth and she spat out a wad of chewed-up flesh that didn't take a whole lot of guessing on my part as to what it used to be.

Randy was laughing; the other man holding her was not. He was humongous. I knew at one glance this must be the infamous Pauly, manhole-rapist. He was staring at that chunk of spat-out penis like he was jealous.

Sandy saw me awaken, her eyes flickering with pain. I got a good view of her face and nearly screamed with rage. One eye was closed and purple and her lips were swollen and cracked.

She was naked, and there were bruises on her the size and shape of men's fists. Her left arm was broken, as well; it hung at a jagged, unnatural angle.

Despite it all, when she saw me, she smiled.

Randy jerked his head in my direction as the guy with the chomped-off penis collapsed to the ground, shaking and cursing, trying desperately to keep the blood from spurting out between his legs.

"I got the girl. Now that he's awake, why don't you go get yours, Pauly?" Randy said.

Pauly let go and tromped over in my direction. He was grinning from ear to ear and was perhaps the ugliest man I'd ever seen.

His head was misshapen, like a football that had gone flat on one side. His right eye hung lower than his left and his nose was almost completely sideways.

He had trouble breathing, and he hissed and huffed as he strode towards me. The rest of him was big, and all muscle. He was bald but for a sad attempt at a Mohawk running down the middle of his head.

Whoever had tried to shave it into fine form had obviously been flustered by the shape of Pauly's skull, because it resembled more a failed attempt at a lightning bolt than a Mohawk. A bit of drool dribbled from the corner of his mouth and I couldn't help but notice the bulge growing between his legs.

The guy on the ground moaned. "You gotta help me, Randy! You gotta!" He held up bloody hands.

"You're the idiot who went and tried to stick your pecker in her mouth," Randy said. He shoved Sandy to the ground and left her, walking over to his friend. He thought her helpless, what with her wounds and that shattered arm. He was wrong.

"I told you she was a wildcat, didn't I?" Randy said, standing over his thrashing friend. "I told you: let's break her arms and legs and punch out her teeth, then we can have ourselves some fun. But you wouldn't listen, would you?"

"She embarrassed me!" the man on the ground cried out. "Now my meat is gone! What am I gonna do?"

Randy produced a pistol that had been tucked down inside the front of his pants.

"You're gonna shut your hole," he said.

The man screamed as Randy placed the gun to his head and pulled the trigger. A blast like dynamite rocked the area, scaring a flock of birds from a tree and echoing around the woods like Armageddon.

The sound stopped Pauly in his tracks. He was two feet from me, his obscene penis practically bursting from his pants. As I was sitting up now, I had an eye-level view. I also had a target.

I lunged forward, jaws snapping. If that move was good enough for my honey, it was good enough for me.

I won't go into details about what happened next. Let's just say there was a lot of blood and a lot of screaming. There was also the lesson that no matter how big you are, you can't stand after your manhood gets bitten off.

Pauly went to the ground, clutching himself just like their companion had. Randy whirled and pointed his pistol at me, cursing like a madman. But Sandy was moving, like I said before, and her teeth chomped on the back of his ankle.

His Achilles tendon popped with a *whang* and Randy spun and fired his pistol into the ground twice.

In the meantime, I was on my feet and running towards Sandy, my hands tied behind my back. I wobbled and almost fell several times, but I managed to stay up until I reached her.

Randy had dropped his gun in his agony and was stumbling off towards the trees to our right. He was screeching as blood gushed from the back of his ankle. He was a few steps from the trees when the first Baby arrived. Randy stopped, stared and cursed again.

It dashed across the ground, slammed into his good ankle, and took him down.

I turned my back to Sandy's and fumbled at her knots. It was no good. I couldn't untie them.

"My boot," I said. I hid dozens of knives all over my body and they surely hadn't found them all. I was right. She crouched down, dug into my left boot, and produced a small, sharp blade. I squatted and she sawed at my ropes with her good hand until they cut enough for me to pull free.

By that time, three more Babies had arrived.

They encircled Randy, toying with him. One chomped on his arm, tearing out a chunk. Another nipped at his ear, taking it off. Randy thrashed around. He was leaking blood everywhere.

I cut Sandy free. She collapsed into my arms.

"We have to go, honey," I said.

Her eyes met mine. She was so tired.

"Okay," she said.

I pulled her up. She staggered in place for a moment but gathered herself. Lying just a few feet away was Randy's pistol. I snatched it up and faced off against the Babies, who had all turned to stare at me.

"Please help me," Randy said.

I shot him in the knee so he couldn't run. He screamed.

Randy wasn't feeling so dandy anymore.

The Babies watched me, uncertain.

"Well, go on," I said. "Compliments of me."

They turned and dove into him.

I grabbed all our gear and put my arm around Sandy. I didn't know how far we'd get before they came after us, but I was hoping the easy kill and easy meals we'd left behind would keep them busy long enough.

It turns out I was right.

"They tracked us," she said, later that night. "They'd been following me for a long time. I led them right to you."

I held her tight. "It's okay," I said.

She was hot. The fever was on her, hard. She shivered against me. I had set her arm just hours before and prayed to God she didn't have any internal bleeding or infections. But there was nothing I could do if she did. It was all a matter of waiting it out.

"That one, Randy, he said they were the last of them. He said all the rest got killed coming after me. Can you believe that?"

I smiled. "Yeah."

"They didn't get me. I want you to know that. They never touched me except to beat me."

"It's okay."

She fell asleep in my arms.

It took a week before she was up and moving again. The Babies never came looking for us and neither did any other humans.

During that week, she told me all about her life before things had changed. I listened. I held her to me. I prayed for her recovery.

In time, she healed.

It was another week when we came upon a big lake. I fashioned a fishing pole and by God caught a nice round of little snappers.

We cooked them over a fire that night and had ourselves a good time. Her bruises were fading and her arm looked a lot better. She smiled a lot and even sang one of her Grease songs for me. It was *Hopelessly Devoted To You*.

I cried at the end of it.

We made love that night for the first time since we were attacked. It was awkward and we were both a bit too tender to do such a thing, but we had ourselves a good time anyway.

Before we went to sleep, I nudged her. Sandy's sleepy eyes opened and she smiled.

"By the way," I said. "You were right."

"About what?"

"My name is Fred."

"Liar."

I shook my head and smiled. "It really is."

"Well, then," she said, her body pressing against mine. "Yabba, dabba, doo!"

We both laughed.

ABOUT THE WRITERS

David Bernstein is a member of the HWA. His short stories have appeared in numerous anthologies and magazines. His novel, Amongst the Dead, will be published by Samhain Publishing, and his novel, Tears of No Return, will be published by Evil Jester Press. He is currently working on a trilogy entitled Machines of the Dead. He lives in NYC and really hates car horns. You can visit him at davidbernsteinauthor.blogspot.com and email him at dbern77@hotmail.com

Vincenzo Bilof lives in Detroit, Michigan, and was recently awarded "Author of the Year" by SNM Magazine for 2011 with eight consecutive stories published for their monthly contests. Additional credits include six stories with Open Casket Press and an appearance in the Frightmares anthology by Dark Moon Books. Vincenzo is also the editor of two anthologies for Undead Press: Cavalcade of Terror and Zombie Tales. His post-apocalyptic zombie novel, Under a Red Sun, is forthcoming from Open Casket Press.

Nickolas Cook lives in the beautiful Southwestern desert with his wife and four pugs and one "not-a-pug". He's the editor of the free online horror e-zine, THE BLACK GLOVE. His fiction and non-fiction has appeared in dozens of print and electronic formats. His novels include THE BLACK BEAST OF ALGERNON WOOD, BALEFUL EYE, DEAD DOG (Max and Little Billy #1), the zombie apocalypse trilogy, CITIES IN DUST and the mashup horror cult classic, ALICE IN ZOMBIELAND, and a recently released short story collection 'ROUND MIDNIGHT AND OTHER TALES OF LOST SOULS.

When he's not reading or writing, he is a student/instructor of the Israeli self-defense system, Krav Maga, and various other martial arts and close combat disciplines. To contact the author see his Facebook page, email him at Nickolasecook@aol.com, or visit him at his official website: THE HORROR JAZZ AND BLUES REVUE.

P. A. Douglas is a full time touring singer-song writer that until recently found out that he had a love for writing. With the debut release of his first novel long past, he's released several new books: Epidemic of the Undead and Watchers.

Check out his website at: www.indie-inside.com

Anthony Giangregorio is the author of 40 novels, almost all of them about zombies, and has edited over 40 anthologies and books. His work has appeared in Dead Science & Metahumans vs. the Undead by Coscomentertainment, Dead Worlds: Undead Stories Volumes 1-7, and Wolves of War by Library of the Living Dead Press. He also has stories in End of Days: An Apocalyptic Anthology Vol. 1-5, the Book of the Dead series Vol. 1-6 by LDP, Zombie Zoology by Severed Press, and two anthologies with Pill Hill Press. He's also the creator of the 10 book action/zombie series titled Deadwater and the apocalyptic series Warriors of the Apocalypse. His action/horror novel Dead Rage is being optioned for a movie at this time. Check out his website at www.undeadpress.com and on Facebook.

Michael D. Griffiths is a man who likes to keep busy. He loves camping in the wilds of Arizona , playing poker, and debating such topics as mysticism, creativity, anarchy, and punk rock. He has worked with Abandoned Towers since its inception, moving from Slush Reader to Market Manager. In the past, his writing has been published in numerous periodicals and anthologies. He was awarded first place in Withersin's 666 writer's contest. He's on the staff of The Daily Discord, Cyberwizard Productions, SFReader, and writes reviews for Innsmouth Free Press. His Skinjumper Series has been chronicled in M-Brane magazine. Living Dead Press has published his novels: The Chronicles of Jack Primus and Eternal Aftermath

Kelly M. Hudson is the author of over two dozen short stories published in a variety of anthologies as well as the author of two horror novels, The Turning and Men of Perdition, both available on Amazon.com. To find out more about Kelly and his work, please visit his website at www.kellyhudson.com.

Daniel Loubier is a relative up-and-comer in the horror genre. "Island Getaway" is the author's second publication under Open Casket Press. His zombie short, "A Family Tradition," was included in, "Dead Christmas: A Zombie Anthology"
His work has also been featured on www.BrutalasHell.com, as part of their short fiction web series. His first novel, "Dead Summit," a zombie horror, was released in 2011. He's currently working on "Exorcising my Demon: The Biography of Eileen Dietz" (Fall 2012). To find out more about the author, visit him on Facebook (Daniel Loubier), Twitter (@DeadSummit), and on his website, www.danloubier.com.

R P Steeves is a former teacher and a writer who specializes in the fantastic. His first novel, an urban fantasy tale of paranormal detection, "Misty Johnson, Supernatural Dick in Capitol Hell" is available in print and ebook formats, and its sequel is due out in 2012.
Follow his blog and learn of his upcoming horror, fantasy and pulp adventure titles at http://www.rpsteeves.com

ZOMBIE BUFFET: AN UNDEAD ANTHOLOGY

Edited by Anthony Giangregorio

If you're hungry for zombie stories, look no further than this anthology.

There's enough rotting meat to satisfy even the most discerning connoisseur, and our all-you-can-eat buffet is sure to please.

Rotting intestines, severed heads and exploding spleens are just some of the courses waiting for you within this book of undead mastication.

So grab a knife and fork, slap on a napkin, 'cause you're gonna get dirty, and prepare yourself for the Zombie Buffet.

A zombie feast of epic proportions.

DEAD CHRISTMAS: A ZOMBIE ANTHOLOGY

Edited by Anthony Giangregorio

Share the most special time of the year with someone you love, or better yet, with an animated corpse!

The living dead love Christmas. Whether they're hanging their entrails like garland, using severed heads like stockings, or hanging body parts like ornaments, even zombies enjoy the most wonderful time of the year.

Santa Claus isn't immune to the walking dead, either.

Zombie elves, killer reindeer and undead hordes, all seek to share in the joy of the holiday . . . and tear Santa apart and feed on his flesh.

So when you grab last year's fruitcake to re-gift to Aunt Martha, just make sure to bring a shotgun, too. Because for all you know, your aunt has turned into an undead flesh-eater, and if the shotgun won't kill her, the fruitcake most assuredly will.

RATS

By Anthony Giangregorio

Killer black rats the size of dogs are roaming the streets and no one is aware of their existence.

Wild dogs, the authorities warn. Stay indoors and all will be fine.

Domenic Salvatore soon finds himself in the middle of a cover-up of epic proportions; where no one will believe the truth.

And why would they? After all, he's just a kid.

What no one knows is that the rats have taken on a taste for human meat, a particular kind of meat actually…young flesh…the flesh of children.

As the kids are hunted one by one, killed and dragged off into the night to be devoured, Domenic realizes that it's only a matter of time before he's next.

Something evil stalks the town of Wakefield, Mass…and it's hungry.

BIGFOOT TALES

Edited by Mark Christopher

The elusive Bigfoot has been a mystery for years.

Truth or hoax? No one knows for sure and perhaps never will.

So does this creature of the forest truly exist? Is there really a missing link that ties together man with his ape ancestors?

Or is it all simply a figment of the imagination.

UNDEAD PRESS

UNDEADPRESS.COM

CREATURE FEATURE
A MONSTER ANTHOLOGY

EDITED BY
ANTHONY GIANGREGORIO

CLAN OF THE BIGFOOT

ANTHONY GIANGREGORIO